The White Lady

The White Lady

Tom Thowsen

Citadell Forlag

Tom Thowsen

The White Lady 2015
Kayaweta 2017
The Curse of Goodness 2018

Translated by Catrine Bollerslev

Fredriksten Fortress, the winter of 1820

The lieutenant observes his reflection in the mirror, noticing his stiff expression behind the thick glasses, brought on by the seriousness of the situation.

"I'll take care of this," he says, running a hand through his blond hair. He puts on his hat and buttons his jacket all the way up before turning around to grab two sharpened flintlock pistols from the table beside him, placing them securely in his belt. He casts one last glance at his reflection – stately and handsome, as per usual.

He puts on a confident face and quickly moves down the staircase in the barracks. The soldiers on guard duty sit with their backs facing him. None of them stir as he passes. Their empty stares are fixed ahead of them, their faces pale and long. He decides to save himself the effort of ordering some of them to join him, choosing instead to pass them wordlessly. He opens the outer door, closes it behind him, and stops on the staircase for a second to look out. His gaze travels down the hill between the barracks, snow beating on the walls along the path. The cold hits him, making his face burn.

The night is still and the moon is shining. There isn't another soul in sight – nor is there a clear indicator that anything is wrong. So why are the guards hesitant to make their way outside? Something out there frightens them. But what? It can't be the prospect of war, ruled out by the union between Norway and its previous archenemy, Sweden. On top of that, the fortress has long since lost its military significance and in a few years, chances are the garrison will be entirely decommissioned.

The imminent decommissioning doesn't worry him. His active duty is due to end in a few months. Before he knows it, it'll be time to pack his things and journey back to his hometown of Trøndelag with his betrothed: the most beautiful woman in Fredrikshald. The inhabitants of the town will be mesmerised when they see her. He just knows it. And it won't take him long to arrange the wedding either. It'll be grander and more magnificent than anything the inhabitants of Trøndelag have ever seen. The tables will abound with mouth-watering meals and excellent beverages; all the most important farmers in the town will be invited. Everyone will see his betrothed in the most gorgeous white silk dress money can be.

Oh, how beautiful she'll be...

Waiting for the wedding is a test in itself. He never would have guessed that a few months could feel like an eternity, but every day, he found himself lost in daydreams. He isn't observant enough, doesn't notice the clear deviations of the soldiers in the regiment.

The commander has already reprimanded him on two occasions, making sure to tell him that he still has a number of weeks left. He desperately wants to avoid a third scolding, so he must fulfil his responsibilities. He needs to show that he can clean up this mess on his own and find out what exactly it is that the guards can't explain... the reason all of them are too frightened to stand sentry at the Bell Tower.

He steps off the staircase by the guard barracks and walks towards the slaves' quarters, the phlegmy coughs of the slaves fighting lung infections growing louder as he approaches. Many are ill with high fevers. Some won't make it through the winter. That's normal in deep winter – nothing to waste energy on. He walks on, completely unfazed.

It doesn't take him long to reach the long staircase that leads to the Bell Tower. He smiles, reminiscing on how exhausting it was to climb the staircase back when he was a recruit. At this point it's second nature, he thinks, as he leaps upwards like a mountain goat. One step at a time. Light on his feet. It takes almost nothing out of him.

The only thing that worries him now is the uncertainty. What is it that's scaring the guards? A ghost? A poltergeist? Or perhaps it is only something harmless and natural?

As he reaches the top of the stairs, an apprehensive pit quickly arises in his stomach. He draws his pistols carefully, loading them as quietly as possible. In spite of his efforts, they produce a sharp, metallic click that cuts through the silence like a scream. He grimaces.

A pistol in each hand, poised to shoot at the first sign of movement, he inspects the space around him. He scrutinises every nook and cranny as he tiptoes along the walls of the citadel. The full moon hangs bright and full above him, covering his surroundings in its dimmed light. The door to the White Bell Tower is open. The entire tower is doused in bright light. He can see as clearly as if it were the middle of the day. But for all it's worth, the tower seems empty.

He enters the tower and looks out the windows. In clear weather, the snow-covered mountains are visible in the distance. Right now, everything on the other side of the Kristiania fjord is covered in a veil of impenetrable darkness. The naked mountain ridges towards the Ringdal fjord are illuminated, shining like eggshells.

The town itself is positioned in the shadow of the fortress. All lights and lanterns down below have long since been put out. Even the partition below the king's bastion is a mass of indistinct grey. He starts forward. Is there something moving down there? He notices something disappearing into the shade of the Powder Tower a stone's throw away.

Lord Almighty! Nobody is supposed to be out at this

hour. Perhaps it's just an animal. Best-case scenario, it's a fox or a badger. He sneaks out of the Bell Tower and down the hill towards the Powder Tower where he stops to listen. Are those whispers he hears in the distance? It sounds like human voices. Could it be his betrothed? She would never … unless perhaps she's in danger? In that case, he has to act quickly, come to her rescue. He's an experienced soldier with sufficient arms and the advantage of surprise on his side. His hands tighten on the pistol shafts, making his knuckles whiten, as he jumps around the corner.

"Who's there!" he demands, right before he stiffens in fear. Right in front of him is a hooded creature with a raised scythe. The sharp blade glistens in the moonlight as the creature stares maliciously at him and says: "Sigurd! Your hour has come!"

He feels his hair stand up under his hat and fails to respond as the creature swings the scythe towards him, knocking the pistol out of his right hand. Panicked, he fires the other. The flint turns a spark, lights the powder in the priming pan, and explodes.

The pistol emits a stream of fire, as a deafening thud rings out between the walls of the tower and the mountainsides, echoing out across the town.

Smoke and sulphur. The smells of hell. And the creature doesn't seem deterred …

The creature swings its scythe towards Sigurd once again. The lieutenant attempts to duck under it, but he isn't fast enough. The curved blade makes contact with his neck. He reaches for his throat, feeling the warm rush of blood streaming through his fingers, unable to breathe.

"Lord," he prays silently, "have mercy on me. Save my soul. Forgive my sins. I don't want to die now. Let me live a little longer!"

The thoughts rush through his head at breakneck speed.

He thinks of his family, his childhood, and everything he holds dear. But most of all, he thinks of her. His betrothed. What will happen to her now? Will she be able to get out of this all by herself? Without his help …

He feels the life drain from his body and he falls to his knees. The world grows quiet around him. An indescribable sense of peace fills him as he floats out of his body and looks down on himself. He hovers above the Powder Tower, his lifeless physical vessel resting limply in the arms of the creature with the scythe.

Death has come to collect him.

And then he sees the light at the end of the tunnel …

Halden, the autumn of 2014

Veronika and I stood on the stairs leading up to our new home, searching for our keys. It was a difficult feat, made infinitely more difficult by the innumerable objects in her bag. We rummaged past her wallet, mobile phone, makeup, nail file, and tampons, not to mention the pens, scissors, old receipts, headache tablets, baby wipes, and other countless useless things she had stuffed in there. Given the state of her bag, it wasn't at all surprising that small objects had a tendency to disappear.

Having turned the bag inside out and emptied it three times over, we felt comfortable concluding that the key wasn't in there.

She looked at me with a pleading expression.

"Are you sure you didn't get them back?"

"Absolutely. You had them last," I said confidently. Her brow furrowed with a combination of frustration and resignation. I did the same thing. It wouldn't surprise me if she had forgotten the keys. She has a tendency to be a little distracted.

I briefly imagined driving back to Veronika's house in Fredrikstad. Three miles both ways. Six miles in total. That would result in more than an hour's worth of wasted time. Valuable time that could be spent working!

Typical, I thought to myself. I was eager to start moving in, overflowing with energy and enthusiasm. I had spent the last couple of months looking forward to this day, when the previous owner would move out and Veronika and I could start setting up our dream home.

I couldn't wait to leave my cramped, worn-out childhood room in my parents' house. It was overrun with dust bunnies and rubbish I had gathered over the years. Piles of old cartoons, schoolbooks, and action films on DVD all over the place.

The hard, narrow bed that ended up giving me back pain.

I wouldn't miss that sorry box of a prehistoric television that should have been tossed years ago, either. Aside from my laptop, PlayStation, and clothes, there really wasn't all that much I wanted to bring with me.

Veronika had been smarter. She had spent the past couple of years gathering things she knew she would eventually need, like décor, curtains, bed sheets, cutlery, and crockery. It was all safe and sound in her parents' attic, waiting for her to move into her own place.

We were both closing in on thirty, so it was about time we invested in a place of our own and it hadn't taken us long to agree that we wanted to stay in Halden. Veronika was a nurse at Iddebo nursing home and I was a car salesman at Glenne Bil.

We wanted to be close to – or right in – the centre of town, from where we would have access to all the facilities Halden had to offer, like the Tista Centre, the Brygga Culture Hall, the restaurants, and the bars. We wanted a place with atmosphere, to be in a beautiful and romantic part of town where our love would have room to grow.

So the choice was obvious: we wanted a house in the Southside, as close to the fortress as possible. I had always loved old houses and that part of town was known for its old wooden structures. The imperial style in Halden had always fascinated me, especially monumental structures designed by Grosch, Gedde, and Garben – like the white bell tower at the fortress. That was their crowning glory. I had once wanted to be a conservationist, but I had long since changed my mind about that.

Finding a house had been more difficult than expected. It had taken time. But we were firm believers that good things come to those who wait and in early May, a house in our price range popped up a couple of minutes from the shopping street. There had been available viewings for the upcoming weekend, which was perfect for us.

We'd driven out at 1pm the following Sunday and parked near the shopping street. The rain had let up and the sun had been peeking out from behind the clouds, making the puddles glisten like shards of broken mirror scattered along the street.

From the roof of the tollbooth, we'd heard the sound of seagulls screeching, and down by the cast iron pillars of the market building, we'd seen a pensioner feeding pigeons.

A few teenagers had exited restaurant Grotten and disappeared into a red Volvo 240, plush dice hanging from the rear-view mirror. My first car had looked just like it and here I was, potentially buying my first house. I'd be lying if I said I had not been nervous. The anticipation of this day arriving was overwhelming.

The house had looked amazing in the advert, and after we traversed the narrow road between the shopping street and the walls of the fortress, we were relieved to see that it looked just as great in person. The street was so steep that the attics of the houses at the bottom were positioned well below the foundations of the ones at the very top.

The moisture from the rain had begun to evaporate, leaving a sweet smell behind in the air. Behind the fence of the neighbouring farmhouse, there was a lilac bush in full bloom. Our house was idyllic in the unique way that only houses in southern Norway could be. The roof and the gutters had looked complete and the façade seemed as though it'd been recently painted. There had been no signs of rotting wood, in spite of the fact that the two-storey house was from 1810.

I had liked the look of the small windows, the double

doors facing the street, and the impressive steps of large granite blocks and black wrought iron railing.

The foreground of the house was framed by a picket fence with an open gate. Before moving inside, we had been invited to have a look around outside. We had come across a neglected backyard characterised by its irregular cobblestones and weeds. Facing the neighbouring house, there was a derelict shed with a rusty tin roof. That said, we had agreed that the backyard had lots of potential if we committed our time, love, and creative skills to restoring its former glory. After that, it would be a great place to host barbeques in the summer. There would be space for a vegetable patch, parking, a pergola for our outdoor furniture, and a fireplace. Both of us were excited before we had even seen the inside of the home.

Just as we had gone to ring the bell, the door had opened and a middle-aged couple conversing with the woman (who was presumably the owner) had stepped out. The couple had thanked her and hurried onwards.

The woman had turned to face us and asked if we would like to come inside.

"We would love to," I had said, following the statement up with an introduction. As soon as we had crossed the doorstep, we had noticed an indistinct smell – the kind that tends to come up in old houses. Moisture damage? Mould? Solidified fats from the kitchen? Embedded dirt in the corners? Regardless, the house had not looked newly renovated. The walls by the entrance had been covered in dark brown wallpaper, which had made the room feel small, despite it actually being a pleasant size.

There had been two doors aside from the entrance itself. One had led into the hallway, the other up to the attic. As the owner had opened the door to the hallway, she had told us we could keep our shoes on. We had followed her into the kitchen, which had been quite large and in relatively good condition. The furnishing had looked worn and out-dated, but the natural colours of the oak had still been fully usable.

Just then, we had heard a flush and the sound of running water. Soon after, there had been a pull on a handle by the entrance and a man in a suit had popped his head in. The estate agent had been a guy around my age. I had seen him around before on account of the fact that he was a bit of a celebrity in town. He was known for being the cheeky party type, with bright blue eyes and a wide smile. A quick conversation and a shaking of hands transpired after his entrance. Soon after, the estate agent had started to show us around 'the museum'. He had told us that the bathroom and the kitchen had been done up relatively recently, but Veronika and I had not found ourselves particularly impressed. The bathroom had been small and cramped, as the shower cabin, the toilet, and the sink had been pressed up against one another. The pink tiles on the walls and the floor had not helped.

The living room had been an adequate size of around twenty square metres and offered two large windows facing the fortress. The floor had been covered with a brown carpet, complemented – in the loosest sense of the word – by brown wallpaper. The room had been furnished with a green plush couch, a dining table, dark bookshelves, and a vitrine with coloured leaded glass.

The whole place had smelled like a smoky pub. There had been a newly washed ashtray on a shelf and a useless vase with red roses on the coffee table.

The bedroom had been the room we were most pleased with – it had been exactly the right size and offered a view of both the Swedish territory and the fjord. We had agreed that we would have to cover the peach-covered walls with

15

a layer of white paint and remove the wall-to-wall carpet. If we were to buy the house, that was …

The attic had been completely empty; we had looked straight at the rafters. There had been windows on each of the gables, but it had seemed the space was just about tall enough to fit a person of 180cm. Best case, we could turn it into a child's room.

In order to get into the basement, we had had to exit the house and enter through the gate to the backyard. There had been an old iron door in the wall and both the door and the wall had been reminiscent of the fortress. Both had been solid, the door in particular. The wall had been around two metres thick with stone steps leading down to the basement, which was shrouded in darkness and had had a floor of packed dirt. There had been a single small window high up on the wall that faced the street, but it had long been covered in dust and cobwebs.

The smell of mould at this point had been overpowering to the extent that we had both been nauseated while in the basement. We had agreed, however, that it too had potential to become a usable space. The fact that we would have to put a fair amount of work into fixing up the house had not deterred us.

In fact, it had left us encouraged. For one, we had figured the condition of the house meant that fewer people would bid on it because people tend to have the same attitude towards houses as they do towards cars - if they smell like smoke and look awful, most of us refrain from making an offer. Our offer had covered the evaluated value of the house, namely one million and six hundred thousand kroner, and no more. To push the owner to make a decision quickly, we had even limited the offer to a twenty-four hour period. I had been told that the house had been for sale at the same price last year.

They had accepted our offer fairly quickly. Veronika and I had been overjoyed, even though it had been miserable waiting for the previous owner to move out. It had taken four months for us to finally move in, so we had tried to make the best of the wait. Days had been spent working overtime, saving each and every penny along the way. On weekends and after work, we had scoured interior design magazines and makeover shows for inspiration.

I had even gone so far as to look into the history of the house, searching through old archives to find the names of a few former owners. I had found documents detailing the entire history of the house since it was erected by the skipper Torolf Andresen. One thing that had stood out to me as I had read through the deeds of the previous owners was that nobody had lived there particularly long. On one rare occasion, an occupant had stayed just over ten years.

The pattern of one short residency after another had stuck until the modern day. The widow from whom we had bought the house had moved in in 1975, making her the person who had lived there longest.

After what had seemed like half a lifetime, moving day finally rolled around. As soon as I was done at work, I jumped into the car and drove straight down to the realtor's office to pick up the key and last pieces of paperwork before I continued on to Fredrikstad.

This key wasn't your standard house key, which would explain why Veronika was so eager to see it when I arrived at her parents' house. It was so large and rusty that it had to be about as old as the house, as far as my untrained eye could guess.

Point is it shouldn't be able to disappear in her bag. So it stood to reason that she had left it somewhere else, which bothered me a little, but I tried to stay positive.

She put all the things back in her bag, and just then, I

thought I heard footsteps approaching. I turned around to look, but there was nobody in the narrow cobble street, lined with old wooden houses.

I had to stop and admire all the details. The small windows with ornate frames, the tiled roofs, and the fenced backyards. Most of it had recently been repainted, but that didn't cover up the scars from old, chipped layers of paint that bore witness to the house's long history. I reasoned that some of the houses were more than two hundred years old.

The noble, deciduous trees at the base of the cliff side were dressed in the beautiful colours of autumn. The Fortress was bathed in the golden glow of the afternoon sun and the Bell Tower overlooked the area from its position on the top of the cliff. Looking up at it practically made your neck hurt.

A chirping voice suddenly rang out over the street. "Oh, Embla, there you are! Come to mummy, my little ray of sunshine."

Silence fell for a brief moment before the door to the neighbour's house creaked open. A woman with a lit cigarette in the corner of her mouth stepped out dressed in light-blue dungarees, a shirt, and white pumps. A white kitten was nestled in her arms.

She fished out advertising brochures from the mailbox, and leaned in the doorframe as she browsed them. After a while, she abruptly glanced in our direction and I nodded at her. She nodded back with a thoughtful expression on her face, most likely trying to remember if she had seen us before. I would have done the same thing. I seemed to remember her face from one of the shops in town.

She took the cigarette out of her mouth and crushed it with the soles of her shoe.

"Hi there! You the new neighbours?"

"That we are." I walked towards her with my hand stretched out. "Frits. And this right here is Veronika."

"I'm Torunn. Welcome to Borgerskansen."

"Thank you," Veronika smiled, turning her gaze towards the white kitten. It rested quietly in the crook of Torunn's arm. "Oh, how pretty you are," she said. Its fur was long and fluffy, and around its neck was a pink silk ribbon. "What's your name, my precious?" She petted it and it started to purr.

Torunn laughed, "Embla."

"Norwegian Forest cat?" Veronika asked, although she already knew the answer. She had had a male cat as a child named Felix. She was keen on getting a new one for our new home – a show cat with a pedigree, worth six thousand kroner.

I've heard it said that a Norwegian Forest cat is kind of like a dog. It follows the owner around the house and wants to be where things happen. A proper cuddly cat. It was a miracle that I hadn't already given in and bought the cat given just how much I loved animals. It didn't make sense to spend that kind of money on a pet now that we had an entire house to renovate.

Veronika's parents helped us out with the fifteen percent we needed in equities in order to get the mortgage. It would've been tough without their help, but now we can put aside some money for the renovations every month.

Much to my dismay, Veronika had embarked on a conversation with our new neighbour. We didn't have time for that right now. Besides, Torunn seemed a bit artificial. Her face was caked in makeup and her dark-blue eyes reminded me of a heavily contoured Cleopatra. She had black corn-rows down to her shoulders and her lips glistened through the pink lip-gloss. I kept my distance and engaged in the conversation as little as possible. I mainly stood around and pretended to be following it. In my mind, I was already fixing up the house. Thankfully, the conversation ended sooner than I had thought it would. That was always something.

The makeup doll disappeared back into her house.

"Women," I sighed. "What now? Do we go back to Fredrikstad, or what?"

Veronika looked at me pleadingly. "Have you checked your pockets? Are you sure the key isn't in there?"

"Oh, wait, it *is* in there!" I found the key in the pocket of my trousers, hiding behind my iPhone. That sort of thing doesn't happen often, but Veronika was over the moon.

"Men!" she chuckled with satisfaction, shaking her head.

"That's enough. Let's get started," I said, unlocking the door. Once inside, I turned to Veronika and said, "She was a little weird, wasn't she? Torunn, I mean."

Veronika stopped. Her dark, doe eyes stared at me as she stroked her auburn locks. She had such beautiful hair that had always kind of reminded me of Jennifer Lopez.

"You didn't like her?" she asked with confusion.

"I don't know. There was something strange about her. I've read that it takes a hundred milliseconds to form a first impression of someone."

"What was wrong with her?"

"I felt she seemed a little artificial…"

"I'd say she seemed artistic. She seemed incredibly nice and interesting. Stop being so conservative, Frits."

I shrugged in response and helped her with her coat.

"It smells a lot better now," I said in an effort to change the topic.

"It really does," Veronika admitted, looking around. It appeared as though everything in the contract of purchase had been respected. The house was meant to be washed and cleared prior to us moving in, so we walked around to make sure that everything was the way it was meant to be. It was clean, but not clean enough for us to start painting.

The wall-to-wall carpets in the living room and bedroom were still a little gross, so we tore them up and threw them out of the window into the backyard.

The odour in the hallway that we had noticed during the original viewing of the house still lingered ever so slightly, but it had to be caused by something else since things were now clean. Possibly from the dirt floor in the basement.

We went into the bedroom, sat down on the floor, and started planning. We ascertained that the floorboards were still intact and all we had to do as scrape off the foam rubber and the remains of the wall-to-wall carpet. After that, we would be able to sand down the wood.

The raised ceiling and its beautiful rosette ornament also appeared to be in good condition; with a power wash and a dash of white painting, it'd be good as new. The same was true for the wall panels and small windows. A loving hand would restore the whole place in no time.

But Veronika didn't seem happy. She furrowed her brow as she fished a hair tie out of her bag. She put it in her mouth as she gathered her hair into a tight ponytail before securing it with the tie. The serious expression on her face didn't evaporate.

"What's up with you?" he asked, embracing her. "You look worried, love. What's on your mind?"

"I don't know…" she started before turning her eyes up towards the ceiling. Her eyes glistened as they filled with tears. She swallowed heavily as if there was a lump in her throat that she had to swallow before she could begin to speak.

"What's wrong, darling? Surely you know what's up?"

She grabbed my hand and looked at me with an almost guilty expression. With a shaky voice, she said: "There's something about this room that I can't quite explain. I just feel unbelievably sad."

"Sad? But we're finally here. You're supposed to be happy."

"I know, but there's a weird atmosphere in here. Some sort of bad energy. I feel like we aren't alone, if you know what I mean…"

"Spirits? You think there's a ghost in here?"

She nodded lightly in response. "I don't know…"

"Aw, poor Veronika," I consoled, putting an arm around her and pulling her closer. I stroked her arm and secretly blamed her weird mood on the supernatural things she liked to watch. Not least that Norwegian series *Åndenes makt*, which is almost exclusively about families who have purchased old houses and come to realise that they're haunted. There's a lot of talk of negative energies and ghosts. Souls who aren't at peace and who haven't crossed over to "the other side".

But I had to respect that she felt this way and not trivialise her feelings. I had to take the bull by the horns, but also take care to not make it worse.

So I carefully continued. "What makes you think so? It's neither dark nor dodgy. Look outside! The sun is shining. It's light and cosy in here. We've bought a romantic house, my love. It's going to look amazing when we're done with all the renovations. You have to stop letting yourself think that kind of thing."

"I guess you're right," she said, wiping a tear from the corner of her eye.

"Of course I am," I said. "But I'll tell you one thing."

"What?"

"I feel like crying, too. Do you know why?"

"No…"

"Because I feel powerless. Especially now that we're up

to our necks in work. Where do we even start? I can't point to a single place in this entire house that doesn't need to be done up. I think that's what's getting to both of us. Powerlessness isn't a good feeling, but I'm sure it'll disappear as soon as we get started."

A smile finally appeared on her face and I couldn't resist the urge to kiss her. I started chuckling gleefully and she did the same as she shook her head. It was all smooth sailing from there and it didn't take long for our imaginations to start running wild. Soon we began to look at the opportunities rather than the challenges and stopped letting ourselves see ghosts in the middle of the day.

"What if we removed the bathroom?" she suggested.

"For what reason?" I said. "Where would the new one go?"

Her question surprised me. I had accepted that we would just have a tiny bathroom. There wasn't all that much space to work with in the old house. None of the rooms were suited for being any smaller.

"What about the basement?" she asked. "We could put the new bathroom down there."

But I couldn't see the basement as a bathroom. It was so unseemly with its dirt floor, cobwebs, and mildew stench. As if that wasn't enough to make me resist the idea, it would mean that we would have to walk outside to get in, since the door to the basement was in the backyard. The idea just seemed unrealistic. I told her as much, and her response surprised me once again.

"We'll just build another entrance. That's all there is to it."

She suggested that we turn the old bathroom into a spiral staircase, leading down to the new bathroom in the basement. We would have space for everything we could possibly want – an infrared sauna, a Jacuzzi, a shower, and a toilet. The walls and floor could have large white tiles and heat cable; the ceiling could be adorned with dimmed lighting and recessed down lights. We could even have a small rattan seating area – a few nice chairs and a round glass table, with candles and red wine glasses.

The idea seemed genius and so we agreed to follow her vision for the new bathroom. I really let myself get carried away.

It didn't take me long to fish out my phone and trawl the internet for the best (and cheapest) bathroom equipment, which promptly brought us back to reality. I knew that it would be expensive, but this was a dream that would end up costing both of us hundreds of thousands of kroner. The furnishing itself wouldn't cost a fortune, but the tiles and all the groundwork – including the heat cables, membranes, and screed – definitely would.

I called up a friend who knew more about that sort of thing than I did and told him about the size of the new bathroom and the condition of the current room.

"You'd be looking at around thirty thousand kroner per square metre," he said, "if you want the job done by a professional who will follow the regulations for wet areas and all that. You would save a lot of money if you did it yourselves," he said encouragingly.

We had eighty thousand kroner in the bank, including holiday funds that hadn't been spent yet. It was a start, if nothing else.

The Situation Escalates

The next day, the doorbell rang. Not long after Veronika had gone to open it, I heard her exclaim "Oh, Torunn!" Great... our neighbour. I was in the kitchen, preoccupied with removing linoleum when the odd woman we had met in the street the day before popped in.

"So nice of you to stop by," Veronika continued. "Come on in. Have a look at what we're dealing with."

"Thank you," Torunn said. "I'm curious, as you know. I've never been in here before. Mrs Nilsen kept to herself most of the time. Never really spoke to her. Just the occasional nod if we happened to see each other."

Torunn had a thermos of coffee, homemade pretzels, plastic cups, and cardboard plates with her, so it seemed like she understood our situation. We hadn't even moved the most basic things into the house; there were two sleeping mats in the living room and that was about it. Before we made our way into the living room, though, we showed her the rest of the house and told her about our grandiose bathroom project. She seemed to like the idea.

"Smart solution," she said excitedly. As we moved around the house, a sceptical look began to settle in on her face. She looked pensive behind the dutiful smile plastered on her lips. There wasn't all that much to be excited by in the house, but when we reached the bedroom she took a step back. She refused to step into the room.

"Oh, yuck! I'm not going in there!" she said, grimacing as though she suddenly felt unwell. She covered her face with her hands and stood still as a statue before Veronika swooped in to help her. Her experience as a nurse had made her so resourceful.

"Are you alright? Would you like to sit down for a bit?"

She propped her up to make sure she didn't keel over.

Torunn nodded.

Veronika and I helped her into the living room and onto one of the mats.

After a few minutes of silence, Torunn began to perk back up. She apologised for what had happened, but offered no further explanation. I began to get suspicious.

She continued as if nothing had happened. Drank coffee, ate pretzels, and spoke about the weather. Told us a little bit about herself, including the fact that she had been living in Borgerskansen for three years. She liked the area a lot because it was calm and, for the most part, the neighbours were nice. On top of that, it was close to the centre of town, which was practical for her considering that she worked in a clothing store in the shopping centre. She loved clothes and was always interested in trying out new fashions. Sometimes she'd change style from one day to the next, she laughed, so there was no cause for concern if we spotted her dressed like a hippie one day and a Goth the next. Other than that, she didn't tell us all that much about herself. She was more interested in us and how we met. I found myself telling her about a time two years ago, when I had participated in a civil defence exercise that had led me and my fictional wounds to the first aid station. I had been put on a stretcher and rushed to the hospital in Halden by an ambulance. The way they had so urgently brought me through the A&E and the way the nurses had responded to me had made it all feel intensely realistic. One of the nurses had been breathtakingly beautiful and I had imagined that Jennifer Lopez was taking care of me because of their resemblance. The blood had rushed through my veins and I felt as though I was on cloud nine. But then she had opened her mouth and uttered a single sentence that had instantly made my blood run cold.

"We're going to have to take a blood sample," she had said with the most stunning smile on her face. Before I knew it, she had stabbed my arm with a needle and I had passed out. I couldn't stand the sight of blood. Afterwards, she had apologised, but things had turned out all right so we parted ways.

The following weekend, we'd bumped into each other at one of the local clubs. She had been out with one of her friends from the hospital, this time outfitting a tight-fitting red dress that had looked marvellous on her instead of scrubs. Not to mention her long hair, loose for the first time, cascading down her back.

Veronika had lit up when she saw me and we had stood around for a while talking about the incident at the hospital. It unfortunately hadn't taken us long to run out of things to say. Aside from the fact that she was a nurse, I had known nothing about her and I hadn't wanted to do too much digging, so it had quickly become clear to me that I would have to act quickly. Desperate to not lose my chance, I had invited her to the dance floor for the Macarena.

After dancing nonstop for hours, we had finally exchanged phone numbers. She had stayed with her friend that night. The last train to Fredrikstad had long since left the station.

I had called her to ask her out for dinner the next morning. She had sounded so kind on the other end of the line and she had immediately said yes. Since then, we have practically spent every living moment together, I concluded, satisfied to see that both Torunn and Veronika were smiling at me. Suddenly, however, Torunn perked up. She looked at her watch and thanked us for our time. Told us she had to be somewhere in an hour, as she stood up from the sleeping mat, picked up her thermos, and made her way to the front door. Veronika followed her out while I went back to peeling linoleum off the kitchen floor. Such a damn hassle. The linoleum was glued onto the floorboards and when it was finally all gone, a trail of impossible-to-remove coconut sacking and glue remained. I had to scrape it off with an old pocketknife I happened to have bought when I was a scout in Kautokeino. The long, wide blade did just the trick.

At the door, the women seemed to be lowering their voices, which made me want to eavesdrop. It was difficult to catch the entire conversation, and I only managed to discern bits here and there.

"I felt that, too. That presence…"

"Souls who aren't at rest."

"Negative energies in the room."

"A suffocating feeling."

"Do you think we'll be able to get rid of them?"

"Why don't you take my business card? Call me whenever and we'll take it from there. We'll leave it at that for now."

When Veronika walked into the kitchen, I said, "Would you please show me that business card Torunn gave you?"

"You still don't like her?" Veronika said, holding out the business card so I could read Torunn Isaksen's address and phone numbers. And her profession, which didn't surprise me in the slightest: MEDIUM, PSYCHIC, HEALER.

"I see."

"What?"

"Torunn is a witch!"

"What? You're calling her a witch? What has she done to hurt you?"

"Nothing at all."

"Honestly, darling. Do you dislike people with supernatural abilities that much?" Her words felt like an accusation.

I decided to explain myself: "Not at all, I just don't want anything to do with them, you know? I think they're con artists who profit off the misfortune of others."

I put the knife down and stood up to give her a hug, but she drew back.

"Why can't you just look at this from a more nuanced perspective? Stop lumping everyone together. The police work with psychics in disappearance cases, and sometimes people with incurable diseases get better with their help. There's more between heaven and earth than what the eye can see, Frits."

"Let's agree to disagree, Veronika," I said to end the discussion before it escalated into an all-out fight. Conversations about the supernatural tended to end up that way, so for the most part, we refrained from bringing it up. This was one of the points we disagreed on. Whereas Veronika believed in all sorts of things, I had a more sceptical viewpoint. There had to be a natural explanation for everything, even if our imaginations sometimes played tricks on us.

She shook her head. "Fine by me," she muttered.

It didn't bother me too much. I was used to her temper by now. Her faith had always varied greatly from mine in more ways than in just the supernatural. She came from a family of Catholics. Veronika went to services at Saint Birgitta in Fredrikstad, where she had been baptised and confirmed. I always thought that must have influenced the way she sees the world, even though she had stopped going to services as regularly as she had used to. In spite of my Humanist background, I had gone to church with her a few times. I had sat on the bench and listened to the priest without feeling much of a connection to anything he was saying. What had surprised me the most each time was how many people still frequented the Catholic church. Unlike the Norwegian state churches, the Catholic church was always filled with people from all over the world. We might differ on the topic of faith, but we had so many other things in common that I never considered it a problem. We loved dancing, walking around in town and in nature, going to concerts, having romantic nights in with good food and wine, and travelling south every once in a while. We loved doing new things together and now it was time to make our dream of sharing a home come true.

The fact that she believed in the supernatural shouldn't be enough to tear us apart, but these recent developments and incidents were the cause of some concern for me. Torunn was to blame. I didn't want her coming in here and making Veronika believe all these things. She would be nothing but trouble.

We had to keep our distance from her.

Outhouses Suck

We didn't see much of Torunn for the next few days, but we did manage to get a lot done around the house. We washed the roof with a thorough power wash, gave the floors a good sanding treatment, and even painted the ceiling in the living room. But then I made my first mistake. Eager to tear down the old bathroom, I turned off the water supply. In hindsight, I should have waited longer to cut off our access to the shower and the toilet…

For the time being, we had to use the shower at my parents' house and, if we urgently had to use the bathroom, we had to resign ourselves to the outhouse. What a nightmare!

The outhouse was located in one end of the shed, which looked like it could come crashing down at any moment. The roof was rusty, corrugated iron and the inside was decorated with ancient photos of King Harald and Queen Sonja, in case you wanted the royal family to keep you company while you did your business.

The times we used the outhouse were rare, but every now and then there was no avoiding it. One day, Torunn's kitten followed me into the outhouse and rubbed herself against my legs before jumping up towards the bench – and straight into the hole. I could hear her scared meows from somewhere down in the dark bin, but it was too deep for me to reach down and grab the poor thing.

I found myself having to reach in from outside of the shed to grab her. Don't ask me how, but finally I got her out and brought her into the kitchen. Veronika didn't know if she should laugh or cry when she saw me walk in with the meowing kitten covered in human waste. I held her as far from my body as possible in an attempt to say clean. Then, I threw up from the smell of waste. Her eyes darted open. "Oh, Frits! What have you done?"

"Don't just stand there!" I screamed. "Do something!"

She rushed towards me. "Put her in the sink."

So there we were. Two adults fighting to clean the kitten before she could tear all our skin off with her claws. She didn't seem to understand that we just wanted to make her nice and clean. What a mess. By the time we had washed and dried her, I was covered in scratches and bite marks.

Despite our efforts, the stench of waste lingered on her, even though her fur had been restored to its original white. Veronika looked at me with a wrinkled nose.

"We have to explain what happened to Torunn."

"Absolutely not! That's completely out of the question. I'm not going anywhere near that witch. We'll just let the cat out into the street and let her walk home from there. Besides, she probably saw what happened in her magic crystal ball."

"Stop mocking her, Frits. You should be ashamed of yourself."

"You're free to go talk to her if you'd like. I have plenty to occupy myself with here."

I knew I was being ridiculous, but I couldn't just let Veronika have her way. I didn't want anything to do with Torunn, so Veronika walked to her house by herself. As it turns out, Torunn took it reasonably well. She wasn't angry. Just amused.

The Bathroom Project Begins

Things began to really kick off three days later. My best friend Jørgen showed up to help us, which was greatly appreciated. A harder-working man would be hard to find. His shaved head, long beard, and heavily tattooed strong arms made him look like the Hells Angel type. The Harley Davidson didn't do much to counteract that impression, but he was easily one of the nicest people in the world.

He was an entrepreneur with all the right connections to get us a heap of professional equipment and fancy machines to make our work easier. Getting good equipment is half the job, so his help was happily welcomed.

The two of us had been best friends since primary school and stayed close all through secondary school. We had always played all sorts of games – a habit which was still going strong. It wasn't unusual for us to play everything from Fifa to Call of Duty until the wee hours.

For a while, we had even played football together. Used to be quite good at it, until we turned fifteen and our hormones started driving us away from sports and towards women. Put it like this: both of us had a fair amount of experience with the fairer sex. My car had seen its fair share of women and the backseat had seen more than its fair share of action. But Jørgen knew to keep that between us. Veronika was definitely the jealous type.

Veronika and her sister, Anne, painted the living room while we started working on the basement. Anne and Veronika are twins, although not identical, so even though they were both stunning, I never mistook one for the other.

Veronika and I secretly hoped that Jørgen and Anne would start dating. We tried in vain to make it happen, but the more we tried, the less interested they seemed to be in one another. In other words, we had to tread carefully. It was best to be quiet about our intentions and try to give them time to figure things out on their own. With any luck, they would eventually fall in love. A restoration project like this just might be the push they needed.

It didn't take long for Jørgen to dish out a good suggestion for the house. Part of the spiral staircase could be built into the concrete wall to save floor space. We used a rotary hammer to make a shaft up to the old bathroom, and removed some of the heavy blocks of stone. We pulled the discarded portions into the backyard using a motorised winch, and before we knew it, the day had passed us by.

I was drenched in sweat when we finally called it a day at six o'clock. My t-shirt stuck to my body and my hair felt heavy and greasy.

Jørgen was no better off. His beard looked like steel wool and his bald head was covered in sweat and dirt. We both needed a shower more than anything, but we still didn't have running water. Instead, we just took off the dirty overalls and hung them up to dry in the hallway.

My shirt was cold and it didn't take me long to change. I put on a grey hoodie, jeans, and a couple of clean socks just as I started to hear voices from the bedroom. Sounded like we had visitors and the new voice seemed familiar.

I looked through to the bedroom and there she was again, chatting away to Veronika and her sister. The Cleopatra makeup and the cornrows hadn't changed, but today she was wearing a flowery tunic and a pair of sandals.

All I wanted to do was sneak off before someone anyone noticed me. Go down to the shopping street with Jørgen. Eat dinner in town.

"There you are," Veronika said, to my horror. "Come say hi to Torunn."

And so, we introduced Jørgen to Torunn. They shook hands and exchanged a few kind words. Almost a little *too* kind. He blushed and a dreamy expression fell on his face. She flashed him a smile of all her pearly white teeth and her voice was thick with flirtation.

"I've heard you're quite the handyman. Entrepreneur and all. Maybe you could help me fix some of the pipes at my house sometime?"

"Pipes, you say? Of course. I'd love to. Really would…"

His sheepish smile was visible even through his thick beard and his snuff peeked out from under his upper lip. They quickly ran out of things to say and an awkward silence ensued.

Veronika turned towards me and said, "You know what?"

"No, what's up?"

"Our house is haunted."

"Ha, ha. Good one."

"It's true. I'm serious."

"No, it's not. Cut it out!"

"Yes, it is. Do you remember me saying that I felt sad when I walked in?"

"Yes, but what does that prove? It isn't that strange. I feel powerless when I see all the things still left to do as well. That's normal."

"No, that's not what it is, Frits. Torunn feels the same way, but unlike me, she can explain where it comes from."

"Is that so?" I turned to Torunn and glowered at her. What a lying bitch! Why was she trying to ruin the peaceful atmosphere with her witchcraft? Veronika was so easily affected by that sort of thing and it scared me a little.

Besides, I hated that Torunn was flirting with my best friend. Worst case, she could lure him into bed and ruin any chance of him and Anne getting together. I had to get her out of our lives before her nonsense brought about too much damage. She truly seemed set on wreaking as much havoc as possible.

"There's a special kind of energy in this house," she said. "Have you felt it?"

"I wouldn't call it special," I answered drily. "We're getting it from Østfold Energi. I can't imagine there's anything strange about clean energy from the Sarp Falls."

"Actually…" Jørgen started.

I looked at him with a confused expression. "Actually what?"

"Your energy comes in from Lærdal, not the Sarp Falls."

"Really? I didn't know that."

Torunn ignored us. What she did next could have been a scene from *Åndenes Makt*.

She closed her eyes and held out her hands as if to receive signals from the spirit world. Veronika and Anne followed her lead and assumed the same position. Jørgen and I found the whole situation embarrassing, to say the least. Jørgen didn't know where to look and I just froze.

With a monotonous voice, she started: "I see a tall, young woman with noble posture. Her hair is blonde. Her dress is long and white…"

"Thank you, that's quite enough!" I said decisively in an attempt to put an end to this insanity. I continued in a milder tone of voice. "We don't have time for that right now. We've been working hard all day and we need to eat." Just like that, they stopped.

"A little food wouldn't hurt," Jørgen admitted without hesitation. He could barely contain his laughter.

Torunn scowled at me, but attempted to soften her expression.

"Fine," she said coolly. "We'll just continue another day."

"I'd rather you didn't," I said. "That's not how we do things around here."

"I see," she said and disappeared before anyone had the chance to sigh.

"Was that necessary?" Veronika said accusatorily. "You couldn't have let her finish?"

"It's all rubbish, love. Have you ever even seen a ghost? I'm ordering pizza."

The rest of the evening passed without further drama and nobody mentioned Torunn or ghosts so much as once.

We sat down in the living room. The white paint had dried nicely, but the room still needed to be furnished. There still wasn't any furniture to boast of, excepting our two sleeping mats. The work lamp had been turned off and we had lit some tea lights in the windowsill and on the floor. All of us gathered around the boxed wine and pizza set up in the middle of the room. The women were browsing YouTube on a tablet. They were particularly fascinated by Katy Perry's *Dark Horse* music video, where she pretended to be Cleopatra while she sang, "So you wanna play with magic. Boy, you should know what you're falling for…" She had plenty of suitors and she turned all of them into sand. What rubbish!

Worst of all, Jørgen was completely lost in the music video, as well. He was lost in his imagination and barely uttered a word. He was probably thinking about Torunn; I feared he was connecting her with Katy Perry. Still, I couldn't help but chuckle when the last suitor was turned into a dog, running around with his tongue out. Running after the princess, just like I feared Jørgen would do with Torunn. He wasn't being himself. It was so unlike him to be this distant. I had never seen him blush with a woman like he had done when she had called him a handyman and asked him to have a look at her "pipes."

None of us said much. We just sat around with our wine and pizza, all of us in our own thoughts. Through the windows, we could see the Fortress. It was dark outside, but it was lit up by spotlights, illuminating the walls like the Soria Moria Castle.

A Difficult Dilemma

Bright and early Saturday morning, Jørgen and I were ready for the next challenge: the dirt floor. The biggest obstacle of them all. The ceiling was only just over two metres tall and we needed at least another metre of space to fit in the polystyrene sheets, crushed stone, and cement. Getting a mini excavator down into the basement was nothing short of impossible, and we didn't have access to a soil vacuum excavator either. It would be too expensive to hire an excavation truck, so we resorted to manual labour. Both of us picked up a shovel and started digging, filling buckets, and emptying them outside.

"We need music for this," Jørgen said, placing a boom box by the staircase leading to the backyard. He put on *Turbo Lover* by his favourite band, Judas Priest, and it almost felt like being at a concert. The sound of the drumbeat melted together perfectly with the guitar riffs in the confined space of the basement.

We played along, using our shovels as guitar just like usual when we played Guitar Hero on the PlayStation. With hoarse voices, we sang along with Rob Halford: "You won't hear me, but you'll feel me without warning, something's dawning, listen then within your senses, you'll know you're defenceless…"

We started digging energetically in time with the music, starting with the corners furthest from the exit so we would still have a decent surface to walk on. With each dig of the shovel, I became more interested in seeing how deep the foundation was. I didn't know if the house was built on the mountain or loose fillings.

Around twenty minutes in, something strange happened.

"Christ on a bike!" Jørgen said from his corner. Or at

least that's what I thought he said, given that was what he tended to say when he was surprised. But Judas Priest was playing too loud for me to actually hear him, so I walked over to turn the music down.

"What did you say?"

"Come look at this!"

I walked over to him, still carrying my shovel. I was braced for the worst, half-assuming that the house was standing on loose fillings, in which case we would need to put a lot more work into it all to make sure the house wouldn't come tumbling down.

Jørgen had dug himself around fifty centimetres down and he had a curious look on his face as he pointed down at his green Wellington boots, towards something flat and even. But I couldn't see what he was talking about so I bent down to have a better look.

"No way! Are those floorboards?"

"Yeah! Isn't that weird?" Jørgen said, jumping up and down on the wood to see if it was stable. "Solid stuff," he concluded with a pleased smile on his face. He spat out his snuff, dug his rolling tobacco out of his overalls, and rolled a cigarette. He lit it, took a drag, and blew the smoke out into the room.

I tapped on the floorboards with my shovel. "Do you think it's a trapdoor?"

Jørgen nodded.

"It definitely sounds like there's a room under there."

"That's incredible." I felt so alive. The child in me was awake and ready to go on an adventure. I imagined a room full of treasures and my entire body tingled with excitement at the prospect of discovering what was under the trapdoor, or the floorboards, or whatever it was we had stumbled upon. I was sure Jørgen felt the same way.

We started to dig like crazy, throwing the dirt on the

other side of the basement floor instead of into the buckets. The hole grew deeper and the mound of dirt beside us quickly grew higher. Finally, we reached the edges, revealing a two-by-three metre trapdoor of thick boards.

"Can you see any hinges?"

"No," Jørgen said

"Maybe it's a manhole cover?"

"Could be. Or maybe there's a potato cellar down there."

"How heavy do you think the trapdoor is?"

"No idea. Let's see if we can get under it."

We grabbed our digging bars and put them under one side of the trapdoor, which turned out to be pressed against a wall.

"Ready, pal?"

"Yes, sir!"

We looked at each other and pushed as hard as we could muster. The trapdoor, heavy as lead, came loose from the surface.

"Hold the bar in place while I put something under it." I found a flat stone and squeezed it in to prop up the trapdoor.

"Great!" Jørgen said. "We can try to lift it up from here."

We squatted down and grabbed the boards with all four hands.

"Lift on three," I said. "One. Two. Three!"

Once again, we used all our power to lift. Slowly, but surely, the trapdoor opened.

"Make sure you don't fall down!" A dark hole appeared and although it was expected, I burst out: "It looks pretty damn deep! Take a step to the side before we flip it. Careful."

We flipped it over and the trapdoor collided with the brick wall with a mighty bang.

The stench of mould hit me when I looked down into

the hole to see a passage. I had no idea how far it continued, but I noticed that the ceiling was made of brick, with small stalactites a bit further down the way.

"Christ on a bike!" Jørgen said once again. "A secret passage? After you…"

"No, no. Guests first and all that. He, he…"

"Alright. If you insist…"

I was relieved to see Jørgen head into the passage first. Sure, I didn't believe in ghosts, but the passage did look dark and narrow.

Jørgen moved slowly down the steep stairs, using the walls to support himself. There was no railing to hold onto, so we had to grip onto the blocks of stone to guide us down. After four or five metres, I felt the floor plateau again. I looked back up the stairs and was blinded by the sun. The halogen lamp shone brightly, but it was no use. The passage was too narrow for the light to shine through. I shuffled closer to Jørgen. Over his shoulder, I could see the start of the tunnel. The archway with the red bricks was illuminated, but the tunnel itself looked like a black hole with a low ceiling. Jørgen had to bend down in order to pass through.

He struck his Zippo lighter. It smelled like petrol.

"Can you see anything?" I asked.

"Yeah, but not much. The tunnel veers to the side."

He started walking and I stayed close behind. It was cold and raw in the tunnel. Jørgen came to a sudden stop, causing me to bump into him.

"What's up?"

"There's a closed iron door."

"Really? Can you see the handle?"

"Yup! I'm trying to pull on the iron ring, but the door isn't budging. I bet you there's rust in the hinges somewhere. Oh, damn it! There's a padlock."

"It's alright, I'll go fetch some of our tools."

I turned around and started back towards the entrance. There was something freeing about walking towards the light, towards the warm, fresh air. Everything came back into view. The ceiling. The walls. The floor. And the stairs felt a lot safer going up.

Before I could blink, I was upstairs. Didn't even need to support myself the way I had needed to on the way down. I jumped past the mound of dirt on the floor, made my way towards the exit, and ran up the stairs and into the backyard where I met Veronika and Anne. They were carrying a bucket full of ceramic tiles from the bathroom between them. They were just about to empty the bucket in the container Jørgen had found. Both of them looked at me in surprise.

"Where's the fire, darling?" Veronika laughed.

"No fire, but come with me for a second. I have to show you something."

"Where?"

"In the basement."

Just then, Jørgen came out of the basement, too. He walked towards the silver-grey company car from Berlingo with a curious smile on his face. He opened the boot and fished out a toolbox, angle grinder, extension cord, and a couple of flashlights that he popped in the pockets of his overalls before passing the rest to me.

"Are you ready?"

"Ready for what?" the women asked at the same time.

"For the treasure hunt," I said.

"Ha, ha. Very funny," Veronika said drily.

"I'm not joking. Just ask Jørgen."

He nodded. "Come on, we'll show you."

And so the four of us walked away from the car. We led the women through the backyard, down the stairs, and into the basement, passing the mound of dirt before stopping by the opening in the floor.

Jørgen turned on the flashlight and shone it down into the passage.

"A secret passage? How cool!" Veronika said excitedly, stretching out her hand. Jørgen handed a flashlight to the sisters and soon after, their excited voices boomed between the brick walls in the passage.

They were back in no time, begging us to open the door.

"Calm down! We're working on it," I said, plugging in the extension cord. Jørgen and I walked back into the passage, each equipped with our own flashlight. He carried the toolbox and I carried the angle grinder and the extension cord behind him.

The cones of light filled the room, allowing us to see clearly. The ceiling, made of brick and the mortar, had begun to sweat lime in the form of stalactites and white lines along the walls and ceiling. The floor consisted of round stones and the iron door was in a dire rusty condition.

Jørgen sprayed the rusty hinges with rust dissolver. He let it sit for a few seconds before he cut straight through the padlock in an elegant, albeit loud, movement. Sparks flew and the passage began to smell as smoke poured out.

In the background, we could still head Judas Priest, now singing the words "You got me locked in!" We sang along at the top of our lungs and pretended we were in the music video, manoeuvring through dark tunnels filled with ghosts and the hottest women imaginable. The harmonious guitar solos cut clean through the air, just like the sharp and metallic sound of the angle grinder. Jørgen went at the door with a crowbar and it opened with a screech.

Talk about heavy metal!

Jørgen beamed, but I couldn't see anything because his muscular body filled the entire doorframe – both in terms of height and width.

"Can you see anything?" I asked impatiently.

"Lord Almighty..."

"What?"

"There's a steep incline. Straight towards the Fortress."

"What?" the women screamed behind me. "Did you say towards the Fortress?"

"It looks like it. Want to see if I'm right?"

"Absolutely! Go on, Jørgen. We'll be right behind you," Veronika said, pushing me further into the darkness. The air was raw and uncomfortable to breathe in.

The plateau transitioned into the steepest set of stairs I had ever seen as we began to walk for what seemed like an eternity. We were deep inside the mountain, which made it feel as if we were in a mineshaft. There was bedrock on our left and brick on top of us as well as to our right. Towards the end, the passage was once again enclosed in brick.

"This is the furthest we can go," Jørgen said. "The passage is bricked up."

"Typical," I said, disappointed.

"Can't we tear it down?" the women asked.

"With our bare hands?" I asked sarcastically.

"With a hammer and a chisel," they said. "We can run back and get them for you."

"Great! Jørgen said. "The toolbox is somewhere by the door."

Half an hour later when they returned with the tools, we began chipping away at a large boulder. It turned out there was soil on the other side of the wall, so we poked a digging bar through the opening to see how thick the layer of soil was. After around half a metre, there was no more resistance and when we pulled the digging bar back through the soil, light appeared on the other side. Daylight!

"We could get caught," I said.

We had to consider our next move very carefully. We didn't quite have our bearings, but it was likely that we were inside the walls of the Fortress at this point. That meant we couldn't just go ahead and make the hole bigger, no matter how curious we might be to find out where the passage led out.

I remembered my grandpa, before his death, telling me about the secret passage between the Fortress and a basement down in the town. It had served as an evacuation route for the officers on duty when the Swedes occupied Fredriksten. Not only that, but the passage was also used to send messengers down with messages and weapons for the civil militia. I had thought about the passage a lot as a child, wondered what it looked like. My grandpa had told me the entrance was by the Bell Tower. Would we finally be able to find it?

A genius idea struck me: we could use my phone! I explained the idea to the others, who all thought it was worth a shot. If nothing else, it couldn't hurt to try.

We expanded the hole in order to fit a plastic tube large enough to fit my phone. Once it was secured, we pushed my phone through to the end of the tube.

Then we made our way back to the basement, into the backyard, and through to the hallway. We all changed in a hurry; Jørgen and I hung our overalls on the hooks outside the front door and locked it. The rain was spitting as we rushed out into the narrow street and Halden smelled like autumn. I looked in the direction of the Bell Tower, standing proud and tall by the grey walls of the Fortress, a veil of mist lingered and blurred the scene.

Something about the autumn atmosphere got to me. The air, heavy with rain, the moist earth, and the smell of rotting leaves all served as a reminder that life is fleeting. That the year was coming to an end. That we all die one day. It made me wistful, although not enough so to detract from my intense curiosity.

We made our way through the cobble streets by the old wooden houses until we reached the walls of the Fortress nearest to us. We disappeared into the gate tower to Borgerskansen and continued on to an old imperial gymnasium named Ekserserhuset. The chestnuts crunched under our shoes as we sped along. The road led us up across the steep slope along a network of twists, turns, and dead ends. Fredriksten must have been practically impenetrable from the town back in the day. The image in my mind of what this area used to be like became clearer as I struggled up the hill, the lactic acid starting to build up. My legs became stiffer with every step. They were as heavy as lead, just like the trap door that had started this whole adventure.

After passing the third gate towards the Fortress, Jørgen started calling my phone. There wasn't another soul around. The only sound we could hear was the rush of the cars down below in town. We took a slight right towards the old bakery and brewery. We stood outside and listened for a little while. No ringtone.

We continued on towards the Bell Tower, passing a Powder Tower on our right, before we reached a plateau – a battery leading to the Powder Tower. We stood by the canons and rested, enjoying the view. It was almost bewitching. The fog was creeping in over the harbour, as though a troll was exhaling cigarette smoke in our direction. The grain silo down on the island of Sauøya looked like a lump of wool.

The pinewood forest behind the silo was emitting steam and the hillsides on the other side of the Idde Fjord along Sweden melted into the water. The borders had been erased by a blurry backdrop that filled the horizon as far as the eye could see. It made the entire northern side of the town disappear.

But the canon we were standing by had a strange history to it.

"You know what?" Jørgen said out of nowhere. He leaned towards a canon with one leg on the mount, holding his tobacco between his fingers as he rolled a cigarette.

"What?" Veronika asked.

"Sometime during the nineteen hundreds or so," he said, licking the rolling paper, "they found a body right where we're standing. Did you know that?"

"It's true," Veronika said. She knew this story. The body of the lieutenant from Trøndelag who disappeared without a trace at the start of the eighteen hundreds.

"There you go," he said, putting the cigarette in the corner of his mouth. He lit it, puffed a few times, and continued. "A lot of people have connected the discovery of the body with the White Lady…"

He was talking about the famous ghost of the Fortress. People had come all the way from the United States for the chance to see her. Some years back, an American production team had even tried to capture her on camera. In vain, of course.

"I know," Veronika said. She and I had gone on a museum tour last year. She had been fascinated by the doll that supposedly resembled the White Lady, along with the story of her and the lieutenant's body. The dismembered remains of the bones had been discovered right where we were standing.

The story was that a lieutenant from Trøndelag, the

49

northernmost part of southern Norway, had disappeared under mysterious circumstances. He had gone missing around 1820, during the changing of the guard. A biting wind had been sweeping the long staircase to the Bell Tower. The new guard had been on his way up to meet Tobias, the soldier he was relieving. He had noticed Tobias faltering, a stiff expression lingering in his eyes. The people in the guardhouse had said the same thing about him. The soldiers had been certain something must have happened. Yet Tobias said nothing. His face had been a ghastly white and his eyes glistened with fear. A tense atmosphere had spread amongst the soldiers, as though evil spirits were haunting them.

While this was going on, the lieutenant from Trøndelag was on the second floor. A little later on, he had come running downstairs to ask if anyone had rope. No one did.

That same moment, they had heard steps outside and the new guard came stumbling in. He was just as pale as Tobias and absolutely paralysed by fear. Not a soul could get a single coherent word out of him either.

Because of these events, the lieutenant had been forced to investigate the matter. What had happened to the soldiers at the Bell Tower? He wandered into the night by himself after he'd placed his loaded pistols in his belt. Half an hour later, the soldiers heard the echo of gunshots along the walls of the Fortress.

The alarm had been raised immediately and the entire crew had gone on a search mission. Again, their efforts were in vain. The lieutenant from Trøndelag was gone without a trace.

Multiple sources confirmed that they had heard a scream that night – a scream that has since been attributed to the White Lady, the lieutenant's partner. Some people had even gone so far as to wonder if she had jumped off the cliff by the Bell Tower after her partner had been shot by a jealous rival.

The lieutenant could also have died by suicide…

Or been shot by his partner…

The two guards who were on duty the next day had information about what had happened that night, but it had been no use. In the aftermath of the events, they chose to keep their mouths sealed. Neither of them had spoken since and within a year of the lieutenant's disappearance, both of them had died. One of them had spent his last days in a madhouse, but Tobias had died in his own home. Both had taken the secret to the grave.

One thing was for sure – the discussion of the case had been heavily fuelled by the discovery of a body buried by the foot of the Bell Tower in 1926. It was, of course, the body of a man. Could it be the lieutenant from Trøndelag?

Who else could it be?

Legend went that the guard at the Bell Tower had been let go after the disappearance. There had to be an explanation as to how someone could bury a body without being discovered. The site of discovery would not have been visible from the town, but it would have been from the bastions in the inner fortress.

Still, the murder – or the murderers, whoever they might be - had not managed to bury the body on the night of the murder. It was theorised that they had stored the body somewhere else while they waited for the perfect opportunity to present itself. If nothing else, the careful dismembering of the body had acted as evidence that some time had passed between the murder and the burial.

Jørgen eagerly continued embellishing. "It's been said that the While Lady shows herself on the brightest nights of spring and summer, so we can relax given that it's autumn. People have claimed to see her on the staircase in the Bell Tower. She supposedly floats; her feet don't touch the hillside. She floats into the forest right by the walls of the Fortress, her long, white dress trailing behind her, arms hanging limply at her sides. Sometimes she turns around and waves as she floats away…"

"Right, that's enough," I said. "Give my phone another call."

We listened. And just like that, we heard my ringtone.

But where was it coming from?

A few steps away, we heard the imitation trumpet fanfare and the synthesiser intro to Europe's *The Final Countdown*. We ran towards the sound.

Inside a nook, hidden from plain sight by the rose-hip bushes, we spotted a hole in the hillside – and my iPhone.

Just to stay safe, we covered the hole with a rock. This was our secret. Nobody aside from the four of us was to know; otherwise the news would spread like wildfire as soon as the press got hold of it. Then Veronika and I could kiss our new bathroom goodbye. I could all too easily imagine our home being invaded by journalists from all over the country, not to mention the town antiquarian, the state antiquarian, and a host of eager archaeologists. We wouldn't have a moment to ourselves. On top of the fact that it would most likely end up costing us a lot of money. I remembered reading that it was the responsibility of the developer to finance an archaeological excavation…

In other words, we didn't have any other choice. We had to hide the secret passage and the faster, the better. So I suggested that we fill it with soil, that way we wouldn't have to carry all those heavy buckets into the backyard. Two birds, one stone.

But the others disagreed.

"Are you crazy?" Veronika said. "That's vandalism of a public cultural heritage site…"

"Exactly," Anne chimed in. "That's a punishable offense."

"I'm going to have to agree with the women," Jørgen said. "As an entrepreneur, this is familiar territory. You're going to have to calm down. You don't have to pay for the archaeological excavation if you find something on your property."

"That's not the problem," I said. "We don't have time for that kind of thing. We'll risk losing the opportunity to use the basement. What will we do then, Veronika? Continue showering at my mum's and using the outhouse in the backyard? Is that what you want?"

I made sure to reassure them that we wouldn't vandalise anything. All we'd do was fill in the opening. Slowly and carefully, of course, to make sure nothing would be damaged in the process. We would place a protective fibre cloth over the whole thing and the polystyrene sheets would protect the structure. The archaeologists probably had their hands full with other excavations, anyway. I made every effort to argue my case.

Veronika and Jørgen seemed convinced, but Anne was stubborn.

"Are you serious? If that's what you want to do, you'll have to do it without me."

It was all a sorry affair. I would have loved for the whole thing to turn out differently. Veronika didn't speak to me about it, or even speak a lot more that day. She mainly just sat on the sleeping mat in the living room and wrote in her diary.

It was obvious Veronika didn't want to talk to me, so I decided to leave her alone and give us both time to cool down. I sat down with my iPhone and browsed Facebook for a while. I wrote a happy birthday message to an old classmate who immediately thanked me like he had been sat around waiting for me to message him. Of course, then I had to check what all my other friends were posting. I liked a bunch of photos - everything from dewy glasses of beer on beaches down south to fancy dinners to selfies to animal videos. I went ahead and posted some photos of our house, including a before and after photo of the living room. I watched the comments, likes, and various emojis roll in.

Around ten o'clock we decided to call it a night, brush our teeth, and head to bed. We both fell asleep almost immediately. Two hours later, I was woken up by a blood-curdling scream. I looked over at Veronika who was sitting straight up, her eyes wide and mouth as open as it could possibly be.

"What's wrong, love?" I asked frantically. "Did you have a nightmare?"

"Did you see her?" she said, voice quavering.

"Did I see who?"

"The woman… She was standing there, staring right at me! The one in the white dress…"

The woman had dissolved after a couple of seconds. Disappeared into thin air, in Veronika's own words.

"It was just a dream," I said, turning on the lights, although it didn't do much to calm her nerves. I made her get up and walk through the house with me, checking every room to show her that nobody was there. Only it didn't go exactly as planned. When we walked into the bathroom, she gasped. "My diary!"

She shook like a falling leaf as she extended her hand and pointed at the corner of the room. It seemed so unlike her to just leave her things lying around like that. She was such an organised person, although sometimes she did get a little distracted. Neither of us understood how her diary had ended up on the dirty floor, exactly where we were planning to build the staircase to the basement. She insisted that wasn't where she had left it. And she was right. I saw her put it down on the windowsill in the living room before we went to bed. I knew she hadn't put it there consciously, but I figured she had just walked in her sleep. She had probably put it there while she was dreaming about the White Lady. That would make sense given that we had all just talked about her.

It wasn't *that* weird…

More Surprises

Over the course of the next week, Jørgen and I finished digging up the floor. The entrance to the secret passage was now hidden from sight and ready to be covered with fibre cloth, but we decided to wait to do so until the following day since it was already past nine o'clock at night. Starving and exhausted, we walked upstairs to meet Veronika. She had removed the last remains of the old bathroom, leaving behind only the tiles and plasterboard. Everything was down to its original state - grey floorboards and pink wallpaper.

She had scoured the walls and the ceiling, which made the room smell like green soap. If it hadn't been for the fact that Torunn was there with her, it would have been the most wonderful sight. She clearly didn't care that I had practically thrown her out of the house last time she was here.

"Oh, hello! Here come the handymen," she said in a suspiciously sweet voice. "Are you done for the night?"

"I guess you could say that," I said. I almost considered going back downstairs and picking up where I left off, but I couldn't resist the urge to be sarcastic with her. "Do you want to help out?" I assumed she didn't, but I was wrong.

"Sure," she said, "but not today. I can do Saturday, though. I'm off…"

"Thanks," I interrupted, "but we'll be fine on our own."

"Hungry?" she said, unfazed by the interruption. "There are open-faced sandwiches in the kitchen. We had a meeting at work today and there were leftovers…"

"Thanks, but…" I wanted to decline the offer, but found myself interrupted.

"Open-faced sandwiches?" Jørgen said. "I love those!"

He smiled wide and looked her up and down, making no attempt to hide the fact that he liked what he saw. Torunn was in all black from top to bottom. Short, black leather jacket. Tight, black tricot. Bulky, black biker boots. She looked like she was ready to hop on the back of Jørgen's motorcycle. I was sure he was thinking the same thing.

Had she dolled herself up for him?

Once again, I found myself wanting to kick her out. I had no interest in her trying to seduce my best friend. I wouldn't be able to stand having her around that often. She would probably come over all the time and try to use her witchcraft on Veronika... convince her that the White Lady is haunting our house. It would accomplish nothing, except making Veronika's nightmares worse.

But there was nothing I could do. The two of them had already hit it off. As far as they were concerned, we stopped existing then and there. Veronika and I faded into the background the rest of the evening. After that, they were inseparable.

A couple of days later, they showed up at the house on his Harley and parked it in the backyard. Both of them were there to help with the renovations, the women upstairs and us downstairs. Business as usual.

We started out with a cup of coffee in the living room and it didn't take long for Torunn to start back up on her nonsense.

"How are you?" She took Veronika's hand and looked intently at her. "Do you still feel the negative energy?"

"Yeah, there's something strange about this house. I've been thinking about it a lot after what you said..."

"I see. Everything will be all right. There are forces with unfinished business in this house. Lots of pain and fear and suffering. I see dark rooms. Violence and murder. I think it might have something to do with the young woman. She speaks to me between her silent screams, when the sorrow and despair let up just long enough for her to communicate. There's something she wants to settle…"

I wondered if Jørgen had told her about the secret passage. 'Dark rooms'?

I shot him an accusatory glance, assuming he had let our secret slip. I wasn't sure if he understood what I meant because he just looked at me with a confused expression on his face before shaking his head and flashing me a strange smile.

"That's enough," I said. "Talk about something more uplifting, please. The sun is shining and it's a beautiful autumn day. Let's focus on boosting our desire work and get some positive energy flowing."

"Let's get cracking!" Jørgen downed the last of his coffee and placed a new pouch of snuff under his upper lip.

Once down in the basement, we started levelling the dirt floor with picks and rakes, making the floor as smooth as possible before putting down the fibre cloth.

"You haven't told her anything, have you?" I asked.

"Oh, no! Are you crazy? My lips are sealed, Frits. Don't you trust me?"

"I do, but…" I had to ask him, just to be sure. "You know, it's easy to say a little too much."

"True, but you have to trust me. Besides, I wouldn't want her to be implicated in any of this, you know what I mean?"

We continued our raking in silence until it slowly became time to go over the floor with a plate compactor to compress the dirt.

I was just about done when Jørgen exclaimed "Christ on a bike!"

"What now?"

"Look!" He pointed at the base of the wall.

My hands shook with excitement and I shoved him aside to squat down for a better look. On a section of wall under the flaky plasterwork, I spotted an arch of red brick. What could it be? A window? A door? An entrance to another room? Or perhaps another secret passage?

We grabbed our shovels and dug down another half a metre to expose more of the wall. There was no sign of a window or a door. The plasterwork was smooth.

"Whoever bricked up this opening did a thorough job," I said, pointing my flashlight at the wall in hopes of spotting an opening but to no avail. If there even was an entryway, it had been perfectly camouflaged.

"They really did…" Jørgen was just as confused as I was. He scratched his beard for a while before he continued. "There have been plenty of fires in this town throughout the years. Looks like they've used the foundations of an older house to build this one. One of my colleagues told me that one of the houses in this area has a basement that leads down to a bunch of other basements under their neighbours' houses… We might be dealing with something similar here."

I nodded, deep in thought.

"You might be right," I said, thinking back to Veronika's and my trip to Rome last Easter. The city was filled with layers of ruins, poking out at all angles.

"Should I get a sledgehammer?" Jørgen asked eagerly. He wanted to try to knock one of the bricks out of place and see if there was anything behind it.

"No, don't do that," I said. "Let me think about it first. Don't mention this to the women yet either, okay?"

"Okay," he muttered, disappointment lingering in his face.

It was all too much. Keeping the secret passage hidden was stressful enough. The prospect of unearthing more archaeological mysteries was a nightmare, even if I was curious. I had to go with my gut on this, so the floor would be postponed a little while longer. There was plenty of other work to do, anyways, like the staircase up to the main floor. We decided it was best to get started on that project in the meantime.

Jørgen and I went upstairs to the old bathroom and drilled a hole in the floor, right where the staircase would be. Then we made our way back down into the basement to check that it looked all right. We dug up an electric jigsaw before walking back upstairs. As we used the jigsaw to break off the floorboards, we discovered that a layer of clay separated the floors. Old-school insulation.

Spent a while discussing what to do with the clay. Removing it would be a huge amount of work. We would have to take down the ceiling in the basement.

We placed a ladder in the hole down to the basement. I stepped down on it and was scratching at the floorboards when I noticed something flat and rectangular in the beams of the ceiling. I reached up and grabbed it.

"A book!" I shouted in my excitement. Just then, I heard the sound of feet shuffling quickly towards the room. Two eager faces looked down at me in the hole to the basement – Veronika and Torunn.

"What? A book" they said in unison. "Let's see!"

Before I could so much as sigh, Veronika had yanked it out of my hands. The two women immediately abandoned the bathroom in favour of the living room to peruse its contents.

"Hey! Wait for me!" I shouted, chasing after the book thieves.

When I came into the living room, they were sitting next to each other on a sleeping mat, flicking carefully through the old book. They were so engrossed in the process that they barely realised I had walked in. I sat down wordlessly next to Veronika. Just then, Jørgen appeared in the doorway. "So this is where you're hiding."

"Yeah, they stole the book from me."

He sat down next to Torunn. Side by side, the four of us read. Rows and rows of the most intricate handwriting imaginable, all written with quill and ink. It was impossible to read. I couldn't figure out a single word on the page. It looked like doodles to me.

"A diary," Torunn said.

As she said it, a shiver went down my spine. I thought back to Veronika's diary – to the night where she had walked in her sleep and put her diary in the bathroom. In the exact same spot where I had found this diary. What a coincidence! I looked at Torunn as she dragged her index finger across the yellowed paper and said, "I think her name was Augusta von Silfverfors. A Swedish noblewoman? Von Silfverfors sounds like something a noblewoman would be called, doesn't it? Hmm…"

She stopped. Stared thoughtfully into the room with something akin to a smile.

"Read more!" Veronika said eagerly. She couldn't sit still. "Come on!" She shook Torunn's arm like she was trying to wake her up. Torunn flicked through the book and read bits to herself here and there while the rest of us waited impatiently. The more she read, the more upset she became.

"Oh no, that's horrible…"

"What is?" I asked.

"Incest."

"Incest? With whom?"

"Her father."

"What? Did I hear that right?" I said. "Her father committed incest with her?"

61

She nodded. "That's what it says."

"I would have chopped his dick off," Jørgen growled, his fists clenched.

Veronika's expression hardened. "Poor woman! That sort of thing makes me so mad; I can practically feel my blood boiling. I have no respect for men like that. None at all!"

"It's disgusting," I said. "We're sitting here with a two-hundred-year-old document written by a victim of incest. A Swedish woman. It's incredible!"

"Yeah. And uncomfortable. Please read more," Veronika said, turning to Torunn who had continued reading while the rest of us talked.

"Relax. Let me skim it first. I have to get used to her handwriting. It's quite pretty. Why don't you make some tea while I read? We can eat afterwards." She didn't lift her gaze from the book for so much as a second.

"Roger that. You have fifteen minutes," I said, standing up. I walked into the hallway to change and it wasn't until then that I realised just how eager we all had been. Jørgen and I had both sat down on the sleeping mats, still in our dirty overalls, and nobody had even noticed.

The more I thought about it, the more I started worrying about the diary in the same way I had worried about the secret passage and the newly discovered door. It was important that we tread carefully; we were toeing the line between legal and illegal activity. That much I knew.

Aside from the fact that I didn't always keep to the speed limit and tended to bring back more alcohol from my holidays than technically allowed under Norwegian law I was a law-abiding citizen. All in all, I considered myself pretty much the average citizen. But keeping things hidden from the most important people in my life left me filled with guilt. I felt vile for keeping Veronika out of the loop when it came to the basement, but I was set on it nonetheless. Things would be easier once we came up with a concrete plan to move forward. Should we break through the wall to see what was behind it? If we did that, Veronika and Torunn would definitely figure out what we were up to. It was probably best to leave it alone…

However we then ran the risk of missing out on something interesting. A hidden treasure was still a possibility. I thought it best to leave the decision for later. Maybe Jørgen and I could reconsider our options a couple of days down the line.

Once we had changed, Jørgen and I went into the kitchen to help Veronika prepare baguettes. The kettle was approaching a boil. The windows were grey with dew, blurring the pedestrians in the street until they looked like ghosts floating past.

I picked up the tea towel to wipe off the window and get a better view. The rain whipped against the window and the brown autumn leaves danced along the pavement. A cyclist in a white rain set hurried down the narrow road right before I heard the screech of her brakes as she swerved an elderly man's wire fox terrier. The man scowled at her as she continued, completely unaffected, while the dog barked at her passing.

"There's so much weird stuff in this house," Veronika said. She shook her head as she placed the mugs on a tray.

Jørgen shot me a strange look.

"Perhaps more than we realise. Right, Frits?"

"I don't know…" I looked back at him as if to say 'if you say anything, so help me God'. I dragged my thumb across my throat, which promptly shut him up.

Veronika turned around and stared at us.

"What's that? Have you found anything else?"

"Not at all. He's just kidding."

She breathed a sigh of relief.

"Good."

When we came back into the living room, Torunn was reading eagerly through the diary. She didn't look up until Veronika announced that food was served.

I placed the tray on the floor in front of the sleeping mat and sat down.

Torunn put down the book.

"Mm, looks delicious." She put her hands on the back of her neck and stretched, supporting herself on the wall behind her.

"Tea or coffee?" I asked.

Her eyes were dazed.

"Coffee, please," she said with a yawn. "It's difficult to read, but incredibly interesting. I'm finally getting used to her handwriting."

"How many teaspoons?"

"Two, please."

I sprinkled in two large teaspoons of instant coffee, picked up the hot water, and filled her mug before handing it to her with a friendly smile. "There you go."

"Thank you so much."

"No worries. Bread's on the tray."

I had been a lot nicer to her now that she and Jørgen were dating. It felt a little weird. I liked and disliked her at the same time. Mainly, I just hadn't adjusted to the way she presented herself – in the sense of her makeup, sure, but more so in the fact that she had to play the role of this psychic medium all the time. Little by little, though, I had managed to get a glimpse of who she was behind the façade. She was a good person - sweet, polite, always soft-spoken, and never angry for long stretches of time. Besides, she genuinely liked Jørgen. Her eyes lit up every time she saw him.

She grabbed a baguette.

"So? How's our incest victim?" I asked as I poured hot water into Veronika's mug.

Torunn didn't react to the question; she seemed a little distant.

"Yeah! Tell us more, darling," Jørgen said with his mouth full of bread. His beard was covered in crumbs.

She took him in and chuckled.

"You're such a mess!" She brushed his beard with a few light strokes before she took a sip of her coffee, leaving the rim of the mug reddened from her lipstick. A sad expression lingered in her Cleopatra eyes. She started talking in a sinister voice.

"I think it's her," she said. "The white lady that Veronika saw the other day…"

And just like that, she reminded me why I disliked her.

"God, just give it a rest! It's all about the supernatural with you, just so you can pretend to be psychic. Stop messing around. Just talk normally."

Her eyes became round. "I'm not messing around. It's true. I can read this out loud to you so you can make up your own mind."

She fell silent for a few moments before asking me a question that made me see red. "Do you believe in life after death, Frits?" She sounded like an evangelist trying to save me from burning in hell.

What the hell did my perspective on life after death have to do with anything? I always tried to avoid discussing religion and politics with people; nothing divides a room like that sort of talk. Despite all of that, I managed to answer calmly. "When you die, that's it. Everything goes dark because you just don't exist anymore… God and all that other supernatural nonsense is stuff we tell ourselves because we're scared of death." I stopped myself there,

65

although I also wanted to add that I think religious people are less intelligent than atheists. Things like that aren't meant to be said out loud.

"Well I believe there's a life after this one," Veronika said. "That we all have a soul."

"Same here," Jørgen said. "I'm sticking to the ideas I grew up with. There has to be a Creator behind all this - something intelligent enough to have created the universe. Things don't just appear out of thin air. Just look at DNA! We're all built on data that must have been programmed by God."

"Exactly. God gave us all souls," Veronika chimed in. "Think about what my uncle learnt when he agreed to undergo hypnosis at the University of Oslo. He floated outside his body and saw himself from an external viewpoint. He even floated through the walls to the neighbouring room and described, in detail, what the psychology students in the room had done and said. Everything he said was true."

"Great!" Torunn said. "Then three of us believe in some sort of spirit world. That's a good start."

I didn't feel like discussing it further. I cared much more about the contents of the diary, so I took a deep breath. Although, I did still want to have the last word.

"But that doesn't mean they necessarily believe everything you say, now does it? No. So keep reading. I'll make sure to offer up a natural explanation at the end."

Darkness fell throughout the house out of nowhere. I looked out the window to see if we were the only ones whose vision had become shrouded by the night, but it seemed as though we weren't alone. The town and the fortress were nondescript blobs under the dark-blue canopy above them. The rain had let up and the full moon was hanging right on top of the Bell Tower.

"Oh, God! Do you think it's her?" Veronika made the sign of the cross.

"The answer's still no," I said. "Can't you hear the wind blowing? I wouldn't be surprised if it's knocked a tree right onto a power line somewhere, love."

"That's not impossible," Jørgen chimed in, as he fished out his rolling tobacco and paper to roll himself a cigarette. Torunn grabbed a packet of cigarettes from her bag.

"We'll light some candles," I said. I stood up and walked to the kitchen to fetch a brown cardboard box of tea lights and candles. Jørgen and Torunn went outside to smoke while Veronika and I lit candles in the living room. We lit as many as we could to make sure the room was cosy. We even brought some of the wooden chairs from the kitchen into the living room to elevate the candles a little.

If it hadn't been for the rush of the autumn wind that made our entire house creek, all the candles might have made the night a romantic one.Instead the atmosphere was tense. The old windows let in a draft and the flames of the candles flickered in the wind. They were almost extinguished when the smokers opened the front door to come back inside. The howling wind slammed the door behind them. I heard the rustling of their jackets as they hung them in the hallway and soon after, they were back in the living room, rubbing their cold hands.

"Dear God, it's windy."

When they finally sat down, Torunn opened the book and said "It's a little difficult to read this since it's written in Swedish from the nineteenth century, but I'll try my best to translate it as I read. How's that?"

"Sounds good to me," I said. "We'd all appreciate it if you did that. Just leave out your creepy voice, if you please."

Veronika nudged my side and glared in my direction.

Fredrikshald, May 7th 1818

The view is wonderful on this lovely spring morning. The still fjord reflects the blue of the sky, framed beautifully by the emerging green on the mountainside. I feel incredibly happy because life is finally starting to look up. I've regained my desire to write. The other day, I bought a diary and a writing utensil, but I until now I haven't had the chance to still down and write. The quill is sharp and sits perfectly in my hand. I love the sound of it scratching against the paper as it immortalises my handwriting. I love seeing it create its wonderful black and white pattern on the page.

I intend to write about what happened this winter, while I still remember it this vividly. I left the Silfverfors estate on February 21st at three in the morning. Everyone was asleep when I snuck out into the brutal winter air. The snow creaked under my boots and the stars shone so brightly in the night sky. Thin clouds of smoke escaped from the houses on the heath, but the windows all were dark. There was not another soul in sight and I didn't run into anyone until I reached Torp. Only then did a horse rush past me, dragging a sled in which I recognised no one. I followed the main road until I reached Lundby. It took me around four hours to reach the coach station, and by then I was exhausted. It came as a relief to be able to take off my bag and relax on the stairs since the station didn't open until nine in the morning. I was the first person there, but they were unloading goods from a sled at Sundquist's, so I gathered up my courage and walked up to the sled driver – a man in his forties with kind eyes and a grey beard – to ask where he was headed.

"Vänersborg," he answered kindly, in response to which

I introduced myself using a fake name, Agnes Hansdotter. I told him I was headed to Gothenburg in search of work and asked him if he would be so kind as to bring me to Vänersborg.

He looked at me for a few moments before flashing his set of darkened teeth and saying, "Naturally, miss Hansdotter. We'll leave in an hour's time."

Then he shook my hand and said, "My name is Birger Larsson. Please take a seat." He nodded towards the sled, took my bag off my hands, and helped me down before he placed the bag at my feet.

He had an old saddleback horse - his stalwart friend who never let him down - to pull the sled. I sat down next to Birger, underneath a warm bearskin rug. It could not keep away the cold as it bit at the delicate skin of my face, burning my cheeks and making my eyes water. I had to squint simply to see. It was worst by the lake, where the wind seemed to get ten times colder and at least five times harsher. The majority of the journey was across the ice. We didn't see land for hours; all we saw were white plains in all directions.

Sometime in the late morning, we finally began to see land in the distance and by the time the first stars began to come out that night, the silhouette of a church tower and windmills appeared between the mountainsides. It was a relief to be in Vänersborg, but a short-lived one, as I quickly began to wonder what to do next. Where would I spend the night? Thankfully Birger, bless his soul, offered me a bed in his cowshed until the snow eased up enough for me to journey on from there.

It was a lonely time, sitting alone with what few animals they had. There were a couple of cows, the old horse, and a sow. I could even hear the cackling of the hens in the hen house. Miserable as it was, it was my own fault, all because

69

I didn't want to be a bother. Birger offered me a place in the living room, which wasn't much larger than my old bedroom, but I turned him down on the offer.

I could tell he was poor and his family didn't have much this late in the winter. They had started rationing from last year's crops; all they had left were potatoes and cabbage. Not a single sliver of meat for the fourteen people in the house, Birger, his wife, their eleven children, and his mother-in-law. As long as they had water and a roof over their heads, they were content. I had bread and ham in my bag, so I had my own provisions. Besides, my sourdough bread was far more tasteful than their bark bread. There wasn't any loneliness to complain about either. I had visitors every time they had to milk and feed the animals.

There were plenty of opportunities to talk and every time, I felt more at ease about fetching water from the well. Dear Lord, the animals drank a lot of water. The cows especially. They drank multiple pails of water every day. I should have known, given my upbringing at the Silfverfors Estate. We must have had twenty cows, if not more. All the same, I had never carried a pail of water in my entire life. My soft and delicate hands weren't made for that kind of work. They were better suited for embroidery and polishing silverware, porcelain cups, and crystal glasses. I had never had my hands dirty either. Never had so much as a splinter in one of my fingers. No blisters on my feet. This was the first time I had any idea what life was like for the common people. I had been raised to become a distinguished housewife and to know how to behave in the company of noblemen and women. I had been raised for a better life. My father, the evil devil who had abused me for years, had big plans for me. He had even found me a husband. A man of thirty-eight, but the most hideous man imaginable. He's a small, greying, thin-haired man with a

70

portly demeanour and a ruddy appearance. His name was Bert Holgerson and my father knew him, as he was one of the landowners from the area.

It didn't help that he was an affluent man with his own castle and properties. No, everything about him made me want to run away. But I had no say in the matter; nobody was interested in hearing my opinion. The wedding was to take place on May 9th in Skara Cathedral. That was what my father and Bert Holgerson had decided. The guest list was long. They had invited the most important people from near and far. I recognised the names of relatives, officials, clergymen, traders, and landowners. The celebration was to last for three days. The whole affair would require thorough preparations, given how much there was to take care of. The tailor had taken my measurements and had begun sewing my wedding dress. It had felt like the rope around my neck was only being tightened more and more. With each passing day, it had become increasingly more difficult to breathe until finally, I couldn't take it anymore. I was on the brink of panic and had to escape. Far away from all the madness!

I braced myself for a life of poverty. Not even the prospect of death scared me after all those years of my father raping me, destroying my self-respect, and making me feel like dirt. He had made me feel like I wasn't worthy of my own life and that I wasn't wise enough to choose someone who was good for me. Wanting to leave all that behind me, I jumped headfirst into the unknown, going wherever destiny took me. The first stop just happened to be a couple of weeks with a poor family while the winter raged on.

Everything happens for a reason, though. I took the opportunity to help the family by buying one of the pigs from the neighbouring farms for them. That way, we had enough meat to get us by until spring.

Time passed on as the snow melted and the lake thawed. The boats finally started sailing again and soon after, Birger drove me to the canal at Trollhätte. The town was teeming with people. It seemed like everyone was headed out on a journey of some sort, making it difficult for me to find a boat with empty space. I walked around for hours trying to find someone to take me with them. I finally happened upon a flat-bottomed riverboat – a bojort filled with rod iron from Kristinehamn - headed towards the sea and out into the rest of the world. They did have to stop at Gothenburg before that, which suited me perfectly.

The captain lit up when he saw me. He seemed like a lovely, open man.

"Of course we'll take you," he said, offering me a cheap cabin on board, which I gladly accepted. I didn't particularly want to stay with the rest of the crew below deck in what I presumed to be squalid conditions. I'd rather shy away from what is like just a roomful of sweaty men ...

He showed me the way to his cabin, placed a blanket over my shoulders, and asked me to sit down on the bed. It was nothing special. The entire room was dark and crowded, with a small sunroof that let in a small sliver of light. But it did smell better than the shed.

"One moment, I'll be right back!" he said, as he rushed out of the cabin with a confused, but friendly expression on his face. I saw the hint of a small smile under his large moustache. It wasn't until then that I asked myself if I could trust him. That was when I realised the nature of the quest I had set out on. I was sitting in a stranger's bed. If he wanted to rape me, he would be able to do so with the greatest of ease since the crew was still on shore. I felt my heart beat faster and started to blame myself for the situation I found myself in. When he returned to the cabin, he was holding a bowl of warm pea soup and pork –

something I hadn't had a taste of in weeks. Even being offered the food with a spoon was a thrill.

"A tasty meal, miss," he said with an expectant look in his eyes. I realised I hadn't introduced myself, so I did. Still using the false name, of course.

"Agnes Hansdotter," I said, thanking him.

"Skipper Hans Olson," he said, lifting his hat. "I hope you'll have a comfortable journey with us, Miss. Hansdotter."

I thanked him once again, dipped my spoon in the bowl, and blew on the soup before bringing it to my lips. It tasted wonderful.

Skipper Olson stood in place for a few moments, looking at me, and then left with a pleased expression on his face. I felt the blood rushing through my veins. I had always had a weak spot for men in uniform. There's something attractive about them and Skipper Olson was no exception. He was so noble and gallant. Young, too. No older than twenty-four and quite a large man with wide shoulders and a powerful build. His coppery hair and moustache were neatly trimmed. His face was mild and friendly, and there was no wedding ring in sight. That made me particularly happy.

I slowly became a little interested in him and started worrying about my shabby clothing. I hadn't had the chance to wash with soap and water for a long time and I smelled just terrible. It wasn't easy to clean myself properly in the cabin, though; all I had to work with was cold water, so I could only manage to rinse myself off and braid my hair.

I was filled with despair. Back at the estate, I would have dressed up in my best dress – the white silk one with the golden neckline that hugged my waist – and my white silk gloves that reached my elbows. Silk shoes would have graced my feet and a gold ribbon would have effortlessly held up my hair. I would have felt like a princess, making the task of charming the skipper the easiest thing in the world. I could have feigned a lack of interest, made the hunter in him chase after me.

But no. I would have to win him over some other way. Maybe I would try to show him my inner beauty and find a way to let him know how caring I am. Use all my wits and charm.

As the afternoon rolled around, the opportunity presented itself. The boat had been moored for a while and nothing suggested that we were due to move soon. We were queuing. There were three boats ahead of us, and the big floodgates had to be opened and closed for each individual boat. Not only that, but the chamber between the floodgates had to be filled or emptied before each departure, depending on which direction the boat was headed. With traffic flowing both ways, it appeared it would be some time before we made our departure.

I took the opportunity to go outside and sit in the shade of a spruce near the floodgates. The hill was covered in dry pine needles and the trunk of the tree provided good support. There was a scrambling in the branches above me and I looked up to see a chipmunk jumping around. I looked back down and fixed my gaze on a hazelnut bush, where the blackbirds were playing in the dead leaves. Just then, I saw him walk towards me with a basket in his hand. He stood before me and explained that we would be experiencing delays, forcing us to push back our departure until the next morning.

One of the floodgates needed repairs. The crew were working their hardest, so all there was left for us to do was wait. He looked as though he was in the throes of grief. A deep frown was plastered on his face, his eyes were small and his mouth was clenched.

But suddenly his face lit up, as though he had just had an excellent idea. He asked if I wanted to go for a walk in the forest for a bit of food and drink. He nodded towards the basket, which was covered with a piece of cloth. I accepted the offer and took the hand he had extended towards me. He pulled me up onto my feet as I thanked him with a smile, before brushing the dry pine needles off my shabby dress. He walked up next to me and offered me his arm, as a gentleman should, and together we walked into the forest.

He turned his gaze towards me and said, "How wonderful of you to join me, Miss Hansdotter. I want you to know that I appreciate it very much."

I tried to remain composed so as to not seem too eager. Still, I couldn't help but feel a little self-conscious. There was something about Skipper Olson that I couldn't quite put my finger on. He seemed so different. Chattier than when I first met him.

We reached a southern-facing meadow with a breath-taking view of the water and sat down next to one another. I snuck a peek into the basket to find two bottles – one filled with champagne and the other with spirit. Nestled between the bottles were fried chicken and bread. The glasses, cutlery, and plates were all in poor condition; they had been borrowed from the boat and their peeling out-sides, accompanied by their scratched insides, testified to many years of abuse. I found myself thinking that even the servants at the Silfverfors estate owned better crockery than this, but quickly reprimanded myself for thinking that way. He had done his best with the resources at his disposal.

And what right had I to complain, I asked myself. By my own design, I had become a poor vagabond, well below his station. Besides, the food and drink looked inviting. I hadn't tasted chicken in weeks and the sight alone made me chuckle with glee.

Skipper Olson grabbed the bottle of champagne and sent the cork flying, the sound echoing like a small gun salute. He pulled out two worn glasses and filled them before handing one to me and toasting to the beautiful view. With a smile upon his face, he raised his glass.

"Cheers!" I said, smiling sheepishly. I sipped at the champagne. It tasted incredible. I let my taste buds revel in the fresh and fruity taste.

"Go ahead, Miss Hansdotter." He pointed towards the chicken and the bread. I placed the champagne down in the grass beside me, and then proceeded to out together a perfect plate. My hands shook from hunger and my stomach growled so loudly that I worried he would hear it. I tried to force myself to remember my manners, but I didn't quite manage. A few minutes later, all the food had been devoured.

But Skipper Olson sat there calm and relaxed, looking at me with heavy eyelids and a smile on his face. He made sure my glass was topped up whenever it dipped to so much as half-empty. As a result, the bottle was finished in no time and it didn't take long before the cork had been removed from the bottle of spirit, as well. The taste was unfamiliar to me. I knew champagne, wine, and liqueur from home because it was served to fancy company, but never anything stronger. At least not to the women... Being drunk was considered incredibly shameful, so no one at the estate drank particularly much. My father abstained altogether and I would never have dared to approach him in a drunken state, God forbid.

The first sip tasted like snake venom. Every millimetre of my mouth was on fire and the liquid burned its way down my throat. My first instinct was to spit it out, but that would have been rude to the Skipper. He swallowed the liquid eagerly. With each glass, he proposed a toast and swiftly proceeded to drink the contents of the glass in a single gulp. He toasted to everything, from a great summer, good health, and happiness, to me and my work to come. He even toasted to his ill mother.

Not wanting to be impolite, I toasted with him and drank. In the beginning, I took care to ensure that there was as little alcohol as possible in my glass, only sipping a little for each toast. But all too soon, the devil's drink took away any hint of reason.

I began to take bigger sips until I was gulping the spirit down just like Skipper Olson. My cheeks became warm and my head began to feel heavy. We laughed loudly and without inhibition, especially when I took it upon myself to speak. My tongue couldn't keep up with my thoughts and the words came out warped, sending us into even more fits of laugher.

Out of nowhere, he grew serious. He stopped laughing and a thoughtful expression fell on his face as he stared straight ahead. His fingers twirled the sides of his moustache. He swayed from side to side, trying his hardest to not keel over. Once he had steadied himself, his stiff gaze fixed itself on my right hand, hanging coquettishly in front of my body, as I leaned forwards ever so slightly. A blissful smile broke on his lips and he grabbed my hand to kiss it.

He attempted to look me in the eyes.

"You know what, Miss Hansdotter?" he asked, the words barely decipherable through his slurring.

"What?" I said, unable to ignore the fact that his eyes were swimming. It was almost as though he couldn't focus on the hand in front of his face.

His head bounced around as he continued. "You're the most beautiful woman," he hiccoughed, "I've ever seen."

Charmed, I turned away and looked at him out of the corner of my eye. I could feel my entire body bubbling with joy as I said, "Stop it, you're just teasing me, dear skipper…"

I had to try to act modest and pretend I didn't believe him. Just to fish for more compliments that would make new waves of lust surge through my body. To make my heart dance for joy!

And the skipper delivered. "Not at all! Trust me," he said. "I know a beautiful woman when I see one. I know women… You have such lovely eyes. And such inviting lips. You almost want to… God. Cheers to your beauty. Good Lord!"

He drank the last glass. The bottle was empty, but we didn't need more anyway. All reason went out the window and I couldn't hold myself back any longer. Our feelings took over. I lifted my dress and straddled him. We kissed each other deeply and greedily.

He threw himself over me like a wild animal and we rolled around in the grass, our bodies as close together as we could manage. He reached for my breasts and began to massage them. I grabbed his hard… But he moaned immediately and practically fell asleep on the spot. It wasn't long before I blacked out either. I have no idea how I made it back to the cabin.

I felt such shame when I woke up the next day. What if someone had seen us? I almost didn't dare to get out of bed. I felt nauseated and dizzy. The anxiety gripped by entire body and I found myself shaking, but I knew that I had to leave the cabin for some fresh air. It took half an eternity to make it up to the deck and a thousand questions raced through my heavy head along the way. What would I say when I emerged? Would they laugh at me or spew sarcastic comments? How would I respond? Perhaps it would be best to laugh with them and pretend to be unaffected. Or perhaps it would be better to apologise and promise that it would never happen again – that I was unaccustomed to spirits and that this would be the first and the last time.

To my relief, my arrival failed to rouse any unwanted attention. The crew were preoccupied with getting the boat into the lock chamber. I was met with nods and a few smiles, but nothing else. Skipper Olson reddened and averted his gaze, pretending not to see me. He disappeared off to the sluice and kept himself busy talking to the workers.

The boat slid carefully into the chamber and the powerful sluices closed behind us. Shortly after, they began to empty the chamber. As the boat sank deeper into the abyss, the stonewalls rose. We went so far down that I had to lean my head back to catch a glimpse of the sky. It felt as though we were in the bottom of a square well.

After a while, they opened the other side of the sluices and we travelled along the high walls. Around five, we were out on the other side and everyone was back on board. The boat glided seamlessly down the river. Once we caught the current, the heavy, rod-iron filled boat was quickly carried away in the direction of Gothenburg and the ocean.

The landscape changed dramatically as we drifted along, – from dense forests to open heaths, to wetlands with golden reeds, cracked by the winter ice. We passed open sandbanks, rock formations, boulders, and rocky beaches. On the banks of the river, there were boats tipped upside down for the winter, as well as those just anchored to the pier. There were boats of all shapes and sizes heading upriver and downriver alike. Some were filled with people who were out fishing while others were almost empty. Some of the crewmembers took it upon themselves to give me a bit of a warning. I was told I couldn't trust Skipper

Olson and that it would be in my best interest to avoid him. He tended to have a weak spot for women and spirits.

Slowly, I began to doubt that he was the right man for me. There had to be some truth to what the crew were saying. At the same time, I refused to believe that he had such a record of seducing women. He was far too shy.

Then again, assuming he drank himself to sleep in every harbour, I could hardly have been the first woman he had attempted to seduce. I decided it would be best to not let him too close or lead him on with false expectations. I couldn't afford to make mistakes like that anymore. Imagine we married and he left me alone with our children while he went out to drink and spend all our money? I hadn't run away to find that.

After a couple days of not talking to him, aside from when it was necessary, we arrived at Gothenburg. Dark clouds loomed like a thick layer of felt above us. The landscape lost its depth and everything only existed in shades of grey, except the eight-sided tower of the Kronan redoubt, built in the seventeenth century to fend off the Danes. The golden crown at the top of the tower glowed against the ominous backdrop. Many claimed that the walls of the tower were twenty-four feet wide and that it was filled with cannon gates. This tower was one of the multiple freestanding fortresses designed to keep Gothenburg safe. The walls of the city had been torn down a few years ago to give the city room to grow, though they had kept the moat in place. It was still visible amongst the houses and tall church towers.

We moored the boat and disembarked. I thanked the crew and headed to the nearest inn to order a beer. I was in a world of my own and sat down at a free table as I thought about my next move. Perhaps one of the servers knew where I would be able to find work in the city?

I had barely sat down before someone grabbed me by the back of the neck and squeezed so hard that it sent shooting pains throughout my entire body. Whoever it was, they held me in place so I couldn't turn around to see them, but I feared it might be my father catching me red-handed to bring me home.

The person leaned closer until their lips were touching my earlobe. "Uh-huh, there you are, you bitch," said a hoarse and unfamiliar man's voice. The sound sent shivers down my spine.

"Please, let me go. It hurts!" I begged desperately, fighting to free myself from his grip. He put me down and when he took a seat next to me, I realised that it was Jens Holgerson – the brother of the man I was supposed to have married. His face was an angry red and he had a crazed look in his eyes.

Paralysed by fear and embarrassment, I just stared at him. I couldn't conjure so much as one sensible word.

He offered me a resentful smile and said: "So this is where you're hiding nowadays? Whoring around, I assume."

The accusation set me off. "How dare you?" I retorted. I couldn't believe he had the audacity to say such a thing and I found myself glancing at the table beside us. The woman sat there was looking at us with a smile on her face. There were two half-empty glasses of beer on the table. She lifted one of them as if to toast with us and I spat back at him, "And you? What are *you* doing here? Who's the girl over there that you must have been sitting with before you came over to manhandle me?"

I nodded towards the woman, who he must have found on the street unless the inn had staff of their own. Although I couldn't quite put my finger on why, I immediately understood that she was by no means the kind of woman that you could be seen with in broad daylight. Best case, she was one of his mistresses.

"I don't owe you any answers," he shot back, refusing to answer. "*You're* going to listen to *me*," he said, making it clear that he intended to continue attacking me. "Do you have any idea how much chaos and concern you have caused? How much shame you have brought on our family? Did you know that your old man, out of pure pain and sorrow – has barely been out of bed since the day you disappeared? His broken heart will not be able to handle much more. Last I saw him, he was nothing but a pathetic shadow of himself…"

"That's quite enough," I said. "Why does nobody care how *I* am or about why I ran away? I hope you know I have my reasons. My father isn't as innocent as people may think. You just ask him yourself next time you see him. I swear on my mother's grave that I'm telling the truth when I say that he took my innocence from me before I was even twelve years old. So you and your brother should thank me for what I've done – for running away before I had to chance to marry into your family… I'm taking care of myself now."

"Shut your mouth! There isn't the hint of truth in your words, you ungrateful slut," he interrupted. His voice almost cracked as he continued. "And how are you planning to care for yourself then? How are you going to put food on your own table? Are you going to become a whore? If you aren't already one, that is."

"God, no!" I said. "How dare you think that about me? I'll find something suitable. Perhaps in a shop or a factory. I'll save up money and open my own shop someday. Become a rich woman. Eventually, I might even move into politics and fight for a better life for the women of this country…"

The idea made him laugh. He had never heard anything so ridiculous. Women in politics? Ha! What on earth did *they* have to say? No, they should stay in their place, far removed from any position of power. He assured me that my feet would get back on the ground as soon as I got a taste of reality and awoke from my naïve dreams. Despite his cruel words, he took out his wallet and poured some coins onto the table. "Here," he said with a chuckle. "Take these and get as far away from here as possible. Go to Africa if you like. Find yourself a Nigerian prince to marry. Or use it to drink yourself straight into oblivion if that suits you better. Either way, get out of here."

That was the end of that. I took the money and left.

I shook like a leaf out in the street while I thought about what to do next. Gothenburg might not be the place for me after all. There were too many people here who knew my family, so it might be in my best interest to leave before I had another unfortunate encounter. But what would I do with myself? In search of a better idea, I went back to Skipper Olson and his boat. Fortunately for me, it was still moored and he was happy to see me.

"Are you coming back?" he said with a spark in his eyes.

"Yes, I am," I said, a little uneasy. I could feel myself blushing, but I knew that I didn't have a lot of options aside from asking nicely if I could continue onwards with them. I had heard them say that they were headed to Fredrikshald in south eastern Norway. Other than what I had read in history books, I knew very little about the town. I knew that Charles XII was shot there in 1718 and that we, the Swedes, had made numerous unsuccessful attempts to conquer Fredriksten Fortress. The last attempt was made in 1814.

Now that we had established a union with the Norwegians, though, I saw no reason I should be unable to find work there, far away from everyone who knew me. When I told Skipper Olson of my new plans, he assured me that I would be most welcome. "How nice, Miss Hansdotter," he said. He seemed genuinely happy to help me back on board and he carried my bag all the way back down to the cabin.

Some of the crew were less excited about my return. I heard one of them mumble, "Well, screw me! Are we really taking her with us again…"

Pure jealousy, I thought to myself as I flashed him a smile.

The next day, we sailed out from the northern coast of Gothenburg. I stood on deck and watched the waves whip against the polished rock formations. It was high tide and white foam coated the crests of the waves. The ocean was dark and looked ominous. Skerries lurked everywhere and crew began to gross tense. There was talk of rosaries and I realised that I was far from the first person to mutter the Lord's Prayer to myself. Though some were struck with fear, others just laughed it off. A young man with minor acne pointed towards a tower on the horizon and declared, "Look! Carlsten Fortress!"

The outburst made one of the older sailors laugh. He was an aging, bald man with a grey beard. "Are we visiting Lasse-Maja?" he asked the young man, who must have been around my age. He smiled back, but said nothing. I had no idea who Lasse-Maja was and it was clear to both me and the old sailor that he didn't either. The sailor's long beard moved with the wind until it crept all the way up by his left ear. Sparks flew from the pipe in his toothless mouth and with another laugh, he took out the pipe and began to explain.

Lasse-Maja, whose given name was Lars Molin, was a thief who dressed up as a woman, hence the name Lasse-

Maja. He was in and out of prison for many years but managed to clear his name time and time again, until he was caught stealing silver from one of the local churches. After that, he was sent to Carlsten Fortress, where he was sentenced to remain for the rest of his life.

The next day, there was nothing but open waters as far as the eye could see. The sails hung limply from the masts as I sat on the deck in the shade of the canvas. Above our heads, the sun was beating down mercilessly and I was beginning to worry that I would tan and ruin my milky white skin. I had no desire to look like a farmer.

I sat there quietly and listened in on the conversations going on around me. Skipper Olson claimed that sailing as we knew it would soon fall out of fashion, as we would soon transition to steamships and end our dependence on the wind. He sighed, adding that such a ship was bound to be in use in Stockholm by the coming autumn. He fixed his gaze on the dark blue ocean ahead. There was barely a ripple in sight.

This lull proved to only be the calm before the storm. As night began to fall, the sky geared up for heavy winds and thunderstorms, forcing us to seek shelter in Smögen, a little past halfway on our journey. It was as though the sky opened up and expelled every drop of rain it had to offer. It poured down for hours. I laid in bed and listened.

The next morning, I woke up to the sun shining through the sunroof, but it was far from a calm morning. Everyone was stomping around on deck and I could hear the crew lifting the anchor and setting the sail. Before long, we were back out to sea, carried forwards by the north western wind. A couple days later we reached the fjord and the Hvaler islands west of Fredrikshald. We continued on to the mouth of the Idde Fjord, or the Ringdal Fjord, as the Norwegians call it.

I stood on deck and let the wind play with my hair, although it was beginning to settle. The air was cool and my fingers developed a mild case of chilblains.

The narrow fjord curved like a dark blue worm between the steep mountainsides, becoming more narrow and treacherous the further in we went. Pine and fir trees were clinging to the cliffs on every shelf and in every crack.

Soon we approached the narrowest part of Svinesund, the sound between Norway and Sweden. Settlements lined the edge of the water on either side of the waterway. The Norwegian side boasted a lovely, white wooden building. There was a ferry moored at the pier, which was teeming with movement from people and horse-drawn carriages alike. I waved and a few people waved back, but it seemed everyone else was preoccupied with the errands of the day.

We glided slowly past the settlement, no longer travelling at full speed. Skipper Olson was always made a point to be careful when he had to be. He had no intention of running aground or crashing into the rocks lurking beneath the surface. It was then when he informed us that if we took any hits now, all the iron in the cargo would bring us down. Thankfully, the fjord widened, increasing the distance between the forest-clad mountainsides and us.

The wind had almost completely disappeared and it slowly became warmer. The rays of sun began breaking through the thinning clouds, and there were seagulls soaring through the air far above our heads, crying in the distance. Ahead of us were more rock formations and islets covered in trees. A section of the fjord cut into the landscape on our starboard side. On our portside, I spotted an enchanting mansion with an English landscape garden with a pavilion and ponds, encircled by large deciduous trees. They told me it was the home of a government councillor named Carsten Tank, who was supposedly one of the most powerful people in Fredrikshald. I glanced back and happened to notice Skipper Olson and first mate Anderson talking to each other at the helm. Anderson seemed a little fired up, as he told the skipper that he had been injured during a run-in with the Norwegians on the morning of August 9th 1814. His face bore witness to the injury; he had severe burns and his nose was gone. With the rain pouring down, the Swedes had attacked the Langnes Entrenchment. There was water and mud everywhere, making the whole situation dark and miserable. Their powder was wet and useless, but the opposition's cannons still worked, which proved detrimental to the Swedish forces. Many died and even more were gravely injured until finally the Swedes had been forced to retreat.

Anderson didn't remember the battle particularly well, but when he woke up in the field hospital, he was told that the cannon he had been manning had been hit by an enemy cannon ball. The fact that he survived was a miracle, but he was always bitter about having been injured five days before the armistice was signed.

"Damn the people in power!" he said. He made no attempt to mask the fact that he thought the war had been unnecessary. The people running the country should bear the full responsibility of every injury and casualty. There was so much death and despair, and for what? "They can go to hell!" he concluded, spitting scornfully over the gunwale.

Skipper Olson agreed. He had been in the navy as an eighteen-year-old, but he had been lucky enough to come out on the other side without any injuries. He described the fighting spirit of the Norwegian navy as almost inexistent. There had been no major conflicts.

My attention slowly shifted back to the views from the ship's deck just as we glided past a handful of anchored sailboats and a barge filled with planks of wood. As we made our way around an islet, Fredrikshald began to materialise at the bottom of a tall cliff. There was a large fortress with a white bell tower at the top. A river streamed through the town and there were plenty of boats moored at the pier. The streets of the town and the paths leading down to the boathouses were brimming with life. Horse-drawn carriages rushed through the streets, loaded with goods. There had to be work for me somewhere here.

The eye-catching stacks of timber told me that there must be plenty of work in town, although a sawmill was hardly a place fit for a woman. I had heard about a cotton mill further upriver by the rapids, so I could always try my luck up there. Regardless, I intended to start looking as soon as the boat was moored.

Once we approached the pier, the sail was taken down and one of the sailors prepared to throw the mooring line. There was a large group of people waiting by the pier, including an elegant gentleman who I assumed to be the businessman who had ordered the rod iron in our cargo. Perhaps he would be able to give me some advice?

He was handsome and well-dressed, so I gathered he must be popular with the women around here. He was wearing a black top hat and a dark blue double-buttoned jacket, topped with a silk scarf. His grey trousers covered the rim of his patent leather shoes. He carried a walking stick and his tight clothing revealed him to be a tall and well-built man. He had dark hair and long sideburns, not to mention large, brown eyes. Had I not known better, I might have thought him to be the twin brother of King Carl John, in spite of the fact that he was much younger than the king. I guessed him to be around twenty-five. God bless Skipper Olson, who was kind enough to introduce me to him as soon as we set foot on dry land.

The businessman was named Olai Enoksen and he surprised me by kissing my hand even though I was in no condition to be met with such a gesture. Quite the opposite, in fact. I felt inferior and unkempt in my most horrendous attire, leaving me humble and withdrawn throughout the entire encounter. Skipper Olson told him about the purpose of my trip to Norway – that I was here to find work. I rushed to add that I had heard of a cotton mill in Fredrikshald and was wondering if it was worth the effort to visit there. I looked at him expectantly.

Olai flashed me a crooked smile. "Oh no, dear, do no such thing. The cotton mill stands to be closing soon as it is. Mads Wiel is a terrible businessman. If it interests you, I can offer you work starting immediately. And lodging too, assuming you need that. What do you say, Miss Hansdotter?"

His dark eyes had an honest look to them as he stood there, taking in my face. A wave of bliss rolled over me and all I wanted to do was shout yes at the top of my lungs and throw my arms around his neck. I was willing to do anything. But before accepting his offer, I had to know what it would entail, even if the relief of having boarding and employment was painted on my face clear as day.

"Oh, that is such good news!" I exclaimed, continuing eagerly. "Thank you, sweet Mr Enoksen. Please, do tell me more."

"Well," he said, "I have a lot of balls in the air at the moment. Rod iron is far from my only business. Amongst others, I own a public house a few minutes from here and I need a server, you see. A fine position, perfect for you. You can live on Borgerskansen, a few streets from here." He pointed towards the settlement of houses by the lowest walls of the fortress, on the steep hill by the bottom of the cliff.

"We can deduct the cost of accommodation from your wages," he said, "if you accept my offer, that is. I can assure you there will hardly be better work to find here in town. You have my word. You're in safe hands, of that much I assure you."

Oh, God is good! He was not only *offering* me work, but practically *begging* me to take it. I thought to myself that it was almost too good to be true, while I considered how much had changed in a few short months. Before I left the estate, the thought of taking on the role of servant would have made me shudder. Now I was willing, if not excited, to accept the work that had come my way.

I accepted the offer and thanked Olai.

Skipper Olson surprised me, though. I think he must have developed feelings for me, poor thing, because there was a hint of tear in the corner of his eye when we said goodbye. His voice even shook a little. He offered me a strained smile under his red moustache, thanked me for travelling with them, and wished me the best of luck. As he took my hand, he gave me a folded piece of paper with his address and a request for me to write.

I looked up at him with a smile as he bowed and tipped his hat to me and Olai Enoksen, who then escorted me to his carriage that was waiting right by the entrance to his boathouse.

What an unbelievable stroke of luck. It must have been predetermined by the Lord above at the beginning of time. Everything seemed so perfect. I couldn't believe that the first Norwegian man I came across had saved me.

He brought me to my new lodgings first. The house was a five-minute walk from the harbour – even less by horse and carriage. Perhaps not, considering the slow ascent of the steep street. Regardless, I said yes to living there and thanked him once again.

The house was the size of the servants' quarters at the Silfverfors estate, although it wasn't quite as old and worn. At least I could live here on my own, as the other rooms were used only for storage.

I had a view of the fjord from my unfurnished room and all the wood in the house was painted in light colours, making it seem bigger than the three by four cubits that Olai claimed the room to be. He promised to acquire a bed for me at some point during the day and he lived up to that promise, as I am sitting on it as I write. It would not surprise me if it had come straight from his own attic given how old and dusty it was. That being said, the sheets, pillow, and duvet are all new. He told me that they would be deducted from my wages alongside the cost of accommodation, which is understandable.

But oh, my God, what a workplace. It has to be the sleaziest public house in all of Fredrikshald. It reeks of smoke and if that wasn't bad enough, it's also dirty and full of questionable guests, mainly old drunkards and frivolous women. Some of the guests are so drunk that they can barely speak.

The innkeeper, Willy, takes care of them. He is nothing short of terrifying, mainly because he is built like a bear. He has wide shoulders and minor rickets, so he waddles when he walks. His beer belly hangs out over his belt and the sleeves of his shirt are rolled up to reveal his muscly arms. Smallpox left scars across his face, but there is something mocking about his smile. His voice is low with a nasal twist, always leaving you guessing about whether he's joking or serious. I hate being near him or even just being in the same room as him, but I've noticed that he tends to laugh after he says something jokingly. It almost seems as though he likes seeing the horrified expression on people's faces when they think he's being serious; that way people

91

know to always be careful when around him. If they aren't careful, he grabs them by the neck and throws them out the door, straight into the gutter. Without a single word.

Yet when some of the guests have the audacity to squeeze my behind, he just laughs. I began to hate him almost immediately, but at least I have work to keep me going for now. Things are looking up more than I had dared hope. Who knows, maybe Olai will have something else to offer me at some point. Something more suitable.

You can always hope. He did say he had a lot of balls in the air after all ...

May 8th 1818

I'm beginning to regret my decision with every moment that passes, my doubts slowly eating me alive.

What have I done?

What will come of this?

One thing is certain: the more time I spend at that damned inn, the more I find out. What I have found out so far does not sound promising. This is turning out to be a nightmare and the whole situation has shaken me to my core.

Dear God, what have I gotten myself into?

They want to turn me into an indecent person. That horrid man, Willy, has been pushing me to do so, and of course, Olai is nowhere to be found. I haven't seen him for over twenty-four hours, but I doubt he's as innocent as he seemed at first. I bet he knows how Willy's running the inn.

This morning, I had quite a confusing experience. I found a parcel on the doorstop, which made me feel uneasy, as it meant that someone had been in my room and placed it there while I was asleep. Who knows how long this person had stood there, staring at me, thinking dirty thoughts as I laid there practically naked. They must have seen my breasts. I feel violated. I'll have to make sure to lock the door from now on and to think twice before opening unfamiliar parcels. You certainly learn from your mistakes. I was too curious to not open it this time. I was confident it was meant for me, given that it was in my room. The package was wrapped nicely in brown paper, with a white envelope placed on top.

After I picked it up, I sat down on the bed, opened the envelope, and started reading:

"Dear Miss Hansdotter. I am giving you this present to show you how much I appreciate having such a beautiful and adorable woman at my inn, and it is my pleasure to reveal that Willy felt the same. I am confident that everything will work out excellently. He said he looks forward to seeing you again.

In this parcel, you will find an outfit that I think will suit you nicely. I hope you like it and that you will do me and our guests the honour of putting it on when you come in to work today.

P.S. The dress is from Paris. I will give you a twenty percent discount on it.

Yours truly,
Mr Olai Enoksen."

Hands trembling, I opened the parcel as fast as I could without ripping the paper. Inside was a gorgeous white, silk dress. It was the epitome of elegant, and even came with matching gloves and shoes. All made from the whitest silk.

I put on the dress and enjoyed my transformation back into a civilised person. I felt like a beautiful swan. I stretched my neck and straightened my back, feeling the person I was just a few months ago begin to return. I started playing around with the thought of telling Olai the truth: that my real name is Augusta von Silfverfors. That I am a noblewoman on the run and that I have chosen to do so to avoid being forced into a marriage with a man I do not love. But could I really find it in myself to tell him?

The thought was appealing. Perhaps he would fall in love with me. You never know. I know that I'm incredibly beautiful when I'm well-groomed, with or without clothes on. I had seen myself naked in the large mirror at the estate every now and then and each time, it had occurred to me that I resembled Aphrodite, the Greek goddess of love. I had long, slim limbs, a narrow waist, and reasonably large breasts. The men just love to stare at me.

It could hardly be a coincidence that the kind Olai Eno-ksen had hired me as quickly as he did without asking whether I had any relevant experience. He quite literally picked me right off the street without knowing anything about me except that I'm Swedish and my name is "Agnes Hansdotter".

My arrival in my new dress roused great attention when I showed up at the inn. Willy's eyes tripled in size as I went to stand by the bar.

He whistled and the only thing he managed to utter was, "Agnes?" The guests turned around to face us and the entire inn grew quiet.

"Yes, Willy," I said, seeing as everyone else is on first name basis with him. "What is it?" I tilted my head and squinted at him.

"Is that really you, darling?" He looked me up and down. "You look like a different person. A beautiful ballerina." His voice was uncharacteristically mild and his eyes were glistening with desire.

"Thank you, dear." I smiled coquettishly. "That's lovely to hear."

"From Olai's collection?" he guessed.

"I would assume so, yes. What gave it away?" I said with a questioning look.

"And I assume the cost of it will be deducted from your wages?" he said with a smile.

"Yes," I admitted, in response to which the giant burst into laughter. The guests laughed with him as I silently cursed myself, wishing I could run away.

They had seen right through me! Of course the dress would cost a fortune, but the thought hadn't occurred to me until just then. It was a degrading moment, made worse by Willy's next question. "And does miss Hansdotter know what the dress costs?

Speechless from shame, I looked into his eyes. It was clear that he was having the time of his life making my life difficult. He had to ask me the same question twice before I finally managed to squeeze out a quiet, "No."

I could feel myself shrinking again.

"Me neither," he said with a chuckle. "But I think you'll have to work for a couple of years to pay that back, sweetie. Olai only sells the most expensive clothes, and to the richest people at that. You have a lot of work to look forward to."

At that news, I fainted. I remember nothing except coming to, lying on a bench inside the inn. There were far too many faces staring down at me and far too many voices buzzing through the air.

Willy lightly slapped my cheek and said, "There, there, sweetie, cross that bridge when you get to it. Have a beer and sit in the back until you feel better. We can talk about the dress later when Olai comes back."

"Do you know when that will be?" I said, choking back tears.

"In a few days," Willy said, scratching the grey stubble on his chin. "He's running an errand in Christiania."

I stayed in the back for a while, wondering how I could be so stupid, but after a couple of beers, I felt less tense. I thought about just how shielded I had been at the estate. I never heard about wages and expenses – that was all for my father to deal with. He gave me what I asked for without telling me what it had cost. That sort of thing has never been for me to worry about.

I knew that we were rich, although I had no money of my own. We never had to buy groceries, which was something that had crossed my mind before running away. I had asked one of the servants to help sell a piece of jewellery – a brooch that I thought must be worth a lot of money. I was right and the money helped greatly while I was on the run. My earnings from that sell lasted me awhile, and thanks to Bert Holgerson's brother in Gothenburg, I still had a fair amount of money left over.

The adjustment to this new life was hard and brutal. A dress can cost so much more than I could ever have imagined, and as a server at an inn, I didn't stand to earn much.

It would take an eternity to pay back the dress, which Willy had no qualms pointing out. He did offer me better-paid work with Asta and Helga. That would involve entertaining some of the more important guests and providing extra services when requested.

It just so happened that these extra services were requested often and that was what caused me to fall in such a deep state of despair. I didn't know much about the whole thing except that it was associated with sin and great shame.

"You damned whore," was becoming a common insult. Aside from Jens Holgerson calling me a bitch and an ungrateful slut, I had only ever heard such insults hurled at other women. The fact that he thought such things about me and had the audacity to say them to my face had really hurt me.

Men are truly strange. They want whores for their pleasure, but use the word "whore" as an insult. Holgerson was *with* one when I met him at the inn in Gothenburg. Part of the reason he paid me to leave was probably that he didn't want anyone to find out.

I must admit I am not pleased at the prospect of proving him right. It saddens me to think that he expects me to fail in my political and commercial endeavours. I don't want to be forced to give up my dreams. To be forced to stop fighting to make them come true.

I can't do that. Surely I should at least be able to marry

an affluent man? To have a family and become a housewife who doesn't need to work. But there's a difference between dreams and reality. My best bet is Olai falling in love with me. If he doesn't, my prospects are bleak at the very best.

He'll be back in two days, so we must wait and see…

May 10th 1818

I'm lying in bed and looking out the window at the clouds floating by. They guide my thoughts back to the sheep at the estate, roaming around without a care in the world. It almost makes me jealous. Sheep don't ask for much in this life; as long as the grass is green, things are fine. None of them want for more and so they never have to make difficult decisions the way people do. They never have to make decisions that might have terrible consequences. I'm debating whether I should keep living in this state of poverty I had neither grown up in nor adjusted to, or choose the quicker route to affluence I struggle to imagine my life without beautiful clothes and things.

Olai and I met in my room after I was done with work last night. He wanted to secure my future by establishing a more binding agreement between us. He had a generous offer for me that I couldn't afford to say no to if I wanted to escape poverty. Things are bleak. I have debts and expenses that gobble up the majority of my wages. Olai thinks it would be a waste for a young and promising woman like myself to miss out on having a proper career. I would regret it for the rest of my life.

Dawn was almost upon is, though darkness still cast the world outside. I had lit a candle on the windowsill, its flickering yellow-grey glow trying its best to light up the room. I sat on the edge of the bed with my feet on the floor and my body cast a long shadow across the room. Olai was sat on a stool in front of me, half the dark.

"You are remarkably beautiful, Miss Hansdotter," he said, attempting to look deep into my eyes. He took my hand.

"I hope you know our customers have taken a liking to

you. Everyone is crowding poor Willy, telling him that they want Agnes."

"No, Mr Enoksen," I said. "You know very little about me. Almost nothing, in fact. I'm not that kind of person. I'm ..." I fell silent for a second for fear of saying too much. All I wanted was to marry rich. I would gladly marry Olai, but in order to do so, I would have to regain some of my previous stature. I had to let him know that I was above this. That I didn't belong in the working class. Yet I still hesitated to tell him.

He continued, "You can confide in me, Miss Hansdotter ..." The words were accompanied by an almost smitten expression. His eyes beamed with warmth and kindness, seeming as though he truly cared deeply about me.

I felt the heat rise to my cheeks as my heart began to race. My walls came crashing down and the tears began to flow. Everything I had been holding back and trying to ignore came flooding back, from how my father abused me for years to how he had attempted to force me to marry a man I didn't love. I told him that my name wasn't Agnes Hansdotter, but that it was, in fact, Augusta von Silfverfors.

Olai fell completely silent and his face softened in compassion as he stroked my cheek to calm me down. "Oh, poor dear! What a life you have had! I'm glad I found you ... May I call you Augusta?"

I nodded.

He handed me a silk handkerchief and sat quietly in front of me as I regained composure. He carefully took my hand and offered me a friendly smile.

His voice was more formal when he spoke again "Dearest Augusta, hand on my heart, I am telling you that you are in the best hands. You can always feel safe around me. Since you have chosen to tell me the truth, I might as well tell you that, from the moment I met you, I doubted that you were a common farmer's daughter coming into town to make your fortune. There was something about the way you speak and the way you carry yourself. The mere fact that you held out your hand for me to kiss. A farmer's daughter would never have done that."

He winked at me and continued smiling.

"Did I do that?" I said. "Did I give you my hand?" I could have sworn he was the one who initiated the gesture, but I suppose it must have been a subconscious move on my part.

Olai continued, a proud expression on his face. "Yes, you did, Augusta von Silfverfors. I saw right through you. I'm not as stupid as I look," he said with a dry laugh.

"Oh, no!" I exclaimed. "I didn't mean it like that. In my eyes, you are as intelligent and handsome as Carl John himself. I pray you don't think that I think otherwise, Olai."

I looked at him intently and gripped his arm.

A few moments later, he said, "Is that so? As intelligent and handsome as the king himself. I appreciate the compliment, although I hope I look younger," he adds. A fair comment, seeing as the king is in his fifties and Olai is hardly older than twenty-five. If the portraits of the king are accurate, though, he has aged incredibly well. There's no sign of wrinkles on his face and his hair has barely begun to grey.

"Of course," I said. "You look much younger, Olai." I was about to tell him that he did not look a day over twenty-five, but he cut in before I could open my mouth again.

"That's kind of you. But perhaps it is time for us to move on, dear Augusta. It's getting late and you have had a long day at work. I am certain you must be tired. Now, I would like to offer you a better position at the inn as a joy girl.

102

You would be earning more in a month than you currently do in a year. With those wages, you could pay your dress back in ... let's see ... seven months. Before long, you would even be able to purchase more dresses, especially seeing as board and lodging would be free."

He continued, "You would eat great food and drink great drinks every day, not to mention meet interesting customers. Some of them are wealthy and powerful people, like business owners, politicians, and actors ... who knows, some of them might even propose. A few years ago, one of my girls married a rich wholesaler from Drammen. As a joy girl, you will get a foot in the door. You never know what could happen. Before you know it, someone may just come around and propose, Augusta."

Still, I refused the offer. The idea of having intercourse with strangers disgusted me. It was impure and sinful, although I would be lying if I said that the money and the rich customers did not tempt me. As Olai pointed out, I am not a virgin. We agreed that I would take some time to think before making a decision. So here I am, counting the clouds until the rooster crows ...

May 11th 1818

The king had his coronation in Storkyrkan in Stockholm. A date to note for him and for me as well. He became the king. I became a whore. Neither of us would ever forget this day. The people would look up to him while they looked down on me. I might as well lie down and die on the stop. Life has lost all meaning now.

May 12th 1818

Things are better now, mostly thanks to the alcohol flow-ing through my veins. I exist in a state of constant intoxi-cation. Good thing, too, otherwise I would not be able to carry out the work I have signed myself up for. Thankfully, I have an almost never-ending supply. I can drink as much as I want at the inn so long as I never drink enough to incapacitate me entirely. It has been going well so far.

I'm usually in a good mood and the customers get what they pay for. I keep them company and let them pamper me. We eat and drink together and I give them all what they want in bed. On that front, things are better than ex-pected. The years of abuse at the hands of my father taught me to distance myself in these sorts of situations. At the end of the day, it is more likely that the alcohol is what saves me from shutting down completely.

I have a wine cellar at the house, which has proven in-credibly convenient. Olai stores wine in such large quanti-ties that he could never keep track of it all. Besides, he told me to take as much as I like.

Because of this, I drink wine with breakfast and dinner. I sleep like a log at night, but my head is always heavy each morning when I awake. My stomach growls and my mouth is dry. Most mornings, I want to eat but feel too nauseated. I always manage to force down some bacon and dry bread, washed down with white wine until feel like myself again. Ready for a new day.

May 17th 1818

Today is Sunday and I think it might be best to stay inside. Bitter feelings have tainted the atmosphere at the inn and in the streets of town as of late. It seems there is some dismay at the state of the union between Norway and Sweden. People have started talking about how the Norwegians were robbed of their independence in 1814 and about the state of the constitution, written on 17 May of the same year. Some of the inhabitants have begun to openly hate everything Swedish, including me. I have found myself on the receiving end of far too many insults lately.

Even Willy has been bothering me. The man is nothing short of crazy. He has no manners and I almost want to alert Olai of the man's coarse behaviour. I am certain he would be fired without further notice.

Today, he sat down with the guests and started up a heated discussion with a group of war veterans. He does that a lot, particularly with the veterans who were with him at Fredriksten in 1814. New stories are sometimes brought back down to Willy, on the rare occasion that one of the men receives mission from the strict commander at the fortress. They sit there and smoke from their clay pipes, telling stories while Willy serves them beer. What was once air is now a cloud of pure smoke. The only thing that breaks through the manmade fog is the paltry candle on the table, trying its hardest to maintain a tiny cone of light amidst the grey. Their rough fists wave among the glasses of beer while their worn voices and laughter drown out every other sound. There seemed to be no end to the stories about missions they had gone on, who had sacrificed most, and who had been injured the most.

One slapped his wooden leg down on the table. The mugs and glasses danced in their places and the candle nearly fell over. "Look at this!" he slurred. "Who can top this?" As if anyone was going to try to compete with his dirty peg leg.

"Did you get gangrene?" someone asked.

"Yes, sir," he confirmed, "Got it from a gunshot wound."

"Wasn't that a few wars ago, Arne?" someone else said.

"Indeed it was. Ten years ago at Prestebakke Church on June 10th 1808. We had attacked the Swedish troops. The devils hid in the church and behind the stonewall around the cemetery. I was almost at the wall when they shot me in the leg and I keeled over. My leg was blown clean off and all that was left was the bone poking out of the wound. There was blood everywhere. I couldn't even move, and it took a while for the others to come to my aid. They carried me into the church, and for the next two days, they used it as a field hospital. I still remember them sawing through my leg as if it was a dry branch they were cutting off or a pig they needed to carve up. I can still smell the blood."

"Blood, you say," a toothless man said. "This thing cost me some blood, too." He proudly exhibited a dent in his forehead.

"What war is that from?" Willy asked.

"The Lingonberry War. Autumn 1788."

Willy suddenly became furious. God only knows what came over him. I had never thought I would see decent people do what he did next, but then again, it might just have been Willy showing his true self — an idiot who should have been behind bars.

The giant slammed his beer down on the table and jumped up. He unbuttoned his shirt, tossed it off, and stood there with his chest bare and heaving. Everyone stared in stunned silence, their mouths open as far as they would go. Had it not been for the one drunkard who laughed, you could have heard a pin drop in the room.

"This is nothing to laugh about," Willy hissed. He looked around the room with a brutal expression on his face and the drunkard put his hand over his mouth.

I was standing by the bar, staring straight at Willy. His entire torso was filled with scars. Then he curtly continued, "The Cat War. Fredriksten Fortress. August 13th 1814." Willy was bitter because of the way his fellow countrymen had let themselves be chased from stronghold to stronghold for two weeks – like a cat chasing a mouse, hence the name.

He sat down and put his shirt back on, but the guests remained silent. Their eyes darted from person to person.

The first person to open their mouth was the man with the wooden leg.

"If I remember correctly, that would mean that your injuries were caused by the Swedish forces' red battery, right? The gunpowder warehouse at Prince Christian's bastion was blown up. One dead, plenty wounded," he said. He went on to express his sympathies for the blood spilled, seemingly in vain. One war after the other. Hunger, distress, and pure misery. In his opinion, Norway would never become an independent nation. The country was doomed to be a province for the rest of time.

August 12th 1818

I am stuck making the most difficult of decisions. I could end up in prison; the solution is strictly illegal, but the problem will not disappear on its own. I have to do something as quickly as possible. The situation gets worse with every day passing day and yet I still find myself uncertain. The voices in my head refuse to leave me alone, making my conscience grow even heavier. They argue their sides. Which decision is the most reasonable? What is in my best interest?

Why should I not put myself first? Why should I not think of my career or my future? But still, it feels like an evil, self-centred decision. My insides scream at me not to go through with it. You will end up in jail. You will resign yourself to perdition. You are an evil witch. I messed up somewhere along the way, possibly I was too drunk when I put in the barrier. And now I've become pregnant. I hate the idea of these 'wise women' poking around my insides.

Asta says they will ruin me.

That I will never be able to have children.

Never become a mother ...

September 7th 1818

"The love of the people is my reward." Such is the king's watchword and it might as well be mine, too. I am indirectly rewarded by men who thirst for love and, in my field, I am the queen that rules over all the other women. I am the only one who wears expensive clothing and though the king's watchword may apply to the entire population, mine does not. Only the highest-paying customers benefit from my expertise; the poor and the working class are of no interest to me. I only work with men from the upper echelons – the ones who can afford me.

The king was crowned for the second time today, first in Stockholm and now in Trondheim. All day, almost everyone at the inn was talking about the coronation and I it seemed to have been a splendid affair. Contrary to usual, it was interesting and educational to listen to the guests today. Since my clients are important people, usually either active in politics or acquainted with people who are, I often hear things that aren't general knowledge. Everyone knows that Queen Desideria lives in Paris and that she was once engaged to Napoleon. The fact that she is in love with the Duke of Richelieu is new information, at least to me. She follows him everywhere and even sends him flowers.

I find myself wondering what kind of marriage the king and the queen have and whether either of them loves each other. I think both the king and I need the love of the people to keep us going. "The love of the people is my reward."

September 18th 1818

Throughout the summer, the most discussed topic has been the tax policies of the Norwegian Storting. The farmers and timber merchants have been hit the hardest, and especially the latter have been seeing a significant decrease in business. Many struggle to simply keep their heads above water. Minor relief is provided to those who are unable to pay their taxes, which must be paid in silver rather than the product of their labour.

Business is thriving for me, though. I have what I need – what more could I want?

September 25th 1818

Today is my birthday, but nobody knows that. I don't want anyone to know either, so that works for me. I don't see the point in life anymore and I am left wishing more than anything that I had never been born. My mother died giving birth to me, and so God knows my father wishes I had never come into this world either.

So what do I even have to celebrate?

October 23rd 1818

I'm going insane and it becomes harder to fall asleep with each passing night. The woman on my left snores like an old man and the woman on my right tosses and turns, coughing her way through the night until sunrise. Somewhere, someone is crying. People are continuously coming in and out of the house to check on how we are doing. There are sounds everywhere – voices in the corridor, voices through the walls, the incessant sound of footsteps.

The room we all share is naked and devoid of even a hint of cosiness. Nothing fills the space but a few beds and a wardrobe. A bright light shines through the large window and straight into my eyes. My whole body aches and the room is unbearably hot. The fever is gripping my body and I'm confident I'll burst into flames at any moment. I can't open the window because chances are, it will do more harm than good to all of us, lying side by side at Fredrikshald's Ebenezer Hospital.

And here I was, thinking it would never happen to me. I began to grow worried when Asta was hospitalised with a venereal disease for the second time within the year. Helga spent all of June and July here and now, it would appear, it is my turn.

October 26th 1818

Willy brought me a lovely bouquet of roses today when he paid me a quick, unexpected visit. He offered me a warm, sincere hug and told me he missed me. Before he left, he wished me a quick recovery.

"Get well soon, beautiful," he said with a smile that revealed his brown teeth. I barely knew he *had* teeth. I couldn't remember the last time I saw him smile.

November 14th 1818

I was discharged from the hospital today, but I'm still not fit for work. Time to rest.

November 26th 1818

Today was my first day back at the inn. I was assigned to the kitchen, helping the cook. I should be able to take on customers again in a few days, although I still feel exhausted.

November 28th 1818

The cook isn't pleased with me and neither is Willy. Both of them claim I'm a disaster in the kitchen, but I must disagree. It isn't my fault that the cook baked such a strange cake, and that he insisted on doing it in a fashion so dangerous that it should be outlawed. For both the health and safety of animals and humans alike.

I had never imagined that things would turn out like this when the cook, beaming with pride, showed me a letter from his uncle in America. His uncle is a cook, too, he explained, and he had sent him some new recipes for dishes we weren't familiar with in the north. To celebrate, he put cake on today's menu.

Fry cakes, he called them. Huge rings of dough, fried in lard with the help of the newest piece of equipment in the kitchen – a strange wood-fired iron oven that Olai had bought in Germany. A so-called *kochmaschine*. The machine cooked the cakes in no time. He stacked them on a tray on the bench, told me to have a taste, and I did. They tasted like lard; the crust was crunchy, but the cake itself was soft.

I ate multiple cakes before the cook stopped me.

"That's enough," he said. "There are other people who want to taste."

I sat down and began to put varnish on my nails, but before long, I heard the cook say: "Can you watch the pot for a while? I have to run an errand."

He took off his apron and disappeared out of the backdoor. I heard the door to the bathroom slam shut just as I realised something smelled burnt. I looked up to realise that the pot had caught fire. I screamed and grabbed the nearest bucket of water in an attempt to put out the fire –

but that only made it worse. A gigantic ball of fire quickly threatened to swallow me whole, and I dropped the empty bucket as I fell over from sheer horror. From the floor, I watched as the flames licked the walls and pipes in the kitchen. There was nothing I could do. I wanted to run to safety, but as I prepared to stand back up, the cook came running in with a blanket. He threw it over the pot and suffocated the flames.

Both Willy and the cook reprimanded me afterwards. It wasn't my fault! Nobody had told me that it was dangerous to throw water on burning lard. I had barely set foot in a kitchen before I came here ... what were they expecting?

December 13th 1818

It feels so weird to be alone in this bed. There's a horse and a sleigh in the backyard and I can hear someone walking around in the basement. The sounds of barrels being rolled around and sacks being stacked rise to my room. They're stocking up. I'm not used to feeling this way on a day like this, but the Norwegians aren't like the Swedes. More precisely, they're not like those of us from the banks of Lake Vänern.

We know how to celebrate this way and my God, the celebrations were beautiful. I have so many wonderful memories of December 13th. The best one must have been when I was around ten years old and my mother's father came to visit. It didn't happen often, seeing as he lived in Bremen on the other side of the Baltic Sea. He was incredibly excited to see me, but I barely recognised him. He looked so different with big bags under his eyes and heavy eyelids threatening to close at any time. His nightcap had slipped back to reveal his now-short hair. In my memories of him, he was always wearing the wig with the long, white powder-dusted ringlets.

"*Wunderschön! Christkindlein!*" he exclaimed when I went to see him in the guestroom, followed by the housekeeper and some of the maids. Dressed in white and carrying silver candlesticks, we walked slowly towards him, moving in time with the words of Santa Lucia. We had flower crowns in our hair and the housekeeper was carrying a nightstand. The maids carried a golden basket of food between them. We served him breakfast in bed and celebrated Saint Lucy's Day. I almost feel like crying.

December 24th 1818

I have never felt lonelier than I do at this very moment. I watched people drink by themselves at the inn all day and it hurt my heart to see them like that on Christmas Eve. Nobody should be alone on the day before Jesus Christ was born. I haven't been to church today, which only leaves me with feelings of guilt. I haven't heard the story of the child who was born in a stable almost two thousand years ago and I haven't heard the familiar sound of the organ guiding us through the Christmas psalms. Then again, it would be hypocritical of me to carry on the religious tradition considering the unholy things I have done this year. I find myself hoping my mother cannot see me from heaven. Her daughter, the whore …

This year, I'm a repentant sinner. I have no partner, no close friends, and no family to speak of. Asta and Helga have gone home to celebrate with their families, but it doesn't feel like Christmas to me. There is no Christmas tree in sight, or any Christmas dinner awaiting me in the hall. There isn't a single festive decoration to speak of and there are certainly no gifts on the way. Actually, that isn't entirely true. Olai gave each of us our gift before the two others left: a silver broche. The only gift I've been given this year. Olai truly has an eye for beauty and always likes to remind us of that. A tradition I have managed to keep up is that of giving others gifts. We always used to give gifts to the poor and my conscience could not let me abandon the tradition. I went down to the shops yesterday, intending to buy some baking equipment for the holiday when I spotted the poor slaves clearing the street of snow. Their chains rattled as they walked along the street.

People in Fredrikshald usually fail to pay any attention to

the slaves that they see every single day. The piteous souls work in all kinds of weather and are considered worthless. They just exist in the fields and forests around us, doing all sorts of hard labour for anyone who wants to rent them.

They're emaciated and scantly dressed in white hats, grey wadmal kirtles with white sleeves, and a grey vest. Their trousers have one white and one brown leg. They must have been freezing in the snow.

I thought to myself that there couldn't be much Christmas spirit in the cold and humid prison cells at the Fortress. All they had for the holiday was water, bread, naked walls, and hard benches to attempt to sleep on. What have they done to deserve this horrible existence?

My thoughts drift back to Lasse-Maja – the man who dressed in women's clothing and stole church silver. He was doomed to spend the rest of his life under these conditions. The story had truly left a mark on me.

I had heard plenty of stories like that one at the inn. The mere act of stealing a slice of bread was enough to get you imprisoned. Only a small fraction of the slaves being kept at the Fortress had committed serious crimes. The murderers were hanged immediately, so there were none of those amongst the slaves.

I meet people from all walks of life by virtue of my profession. Aside from the king, I think I must be one of the people in the country that hears the most stories. I often find myself in close quarters with people others never speak to, hearing confidential stories day in and day out. After some beers and a few rounds in bed, some of the most influential people in our society often end up telling me a story or two. It doesn't take any prying before they open up to me, just as they would if I was one of their closest friends.

One of them told me he used to be an executioner. The

121

phrase was uttered so nonchalantly that the sip of champagne I had just taken nearly went down the wrong way. He had invited me to some of the best restaurants in town, which was far from unusual behaviour amongst my customers. Olai's inn is nothing to write home about. Nobody worth anything sits down for a meal there, so nights out at other establishments were not uncommon.

Because of my work, I had come to understand and read people fairly easily. It was plain to see that this man was melancholy; his face was so stiff, it might as well have been carved from stone. His demeanour was serious, highlighted by his dead eyes. I got the impression that he was the kind of person who would never smile unless you tickled the soles of his feet, and that was assuming he was even ticklish. That being said, had I been in his shoes, I am certain I would look just as grave. His character roused curiosity and so I asked him as many questions as possible.

He resented the developments in legislation. "The punishments criminals face now are far more lenient," he lamented. In his opinion, the laws that came into effect in 1815 should never even have been up for discussion. He firmly believed torture should be reinstated. Now, murderers were all decapitated with axes rather than being punished using methods that would scar them forever, like in the good old days. Back then, everyone got what they deserved, whether it was by dismemberment or poking with red-hot iron prongs. Criminals deserved to suffer a painful death.

I asked him if the memories haunted him.

"No," he answered, although he amended his answer after a few moments of silence. "Some of them."

He confessed that sometimes he wakes up in the middle of the night, soaking wet from sweat. Occurrences like that were rare, he claims, and most nights he slept just fine. The memories did not weight heavily on his conscience. Although I refrained from saying it out loud, I doubted that that was true. Had he seen himself in the mirror, he would have thought the same thing.

The memories of Lasse-Maja, the executioner, and all the other stories I had heard over the course of the past year drove me to do something kind for the slaves clearing the streets of snow. I went to the bakery and bought all the Christmas pastries they had in the shop. It was expensive, but worth it. I will never forget the joy on their faces. Many of them cried out "God bless you", others just wept.

April 15th 1819

I'm sitting here, looking out the window. The sun has started rising earlier now that spring has arrived. The sun is already beating down from above, and the glistening fjord behind Sauøya is reflecting the Swedish mountains. The white sails of the ships approaching Svinesund stretch out as if they were on a clothesline. I've opened the window to air out the room, which still smells of the linseed oil I used to paint the windowsill yesterday. In preparation for spring, I've put up new lace curtains that truly have given the room a bit of a makeover. After all this time, this place is finally beginning to look like a home.

Some purchases I made last autumn when I was ill have finally come in. Olai secured some French furniture for me, every piece made from dark mahogany. There's even a tall mirror so I can see my whole body at the same time, plus a large wardrobe for my clothes. Not only that, but there are also four dining room chairs with a matching oval table. Everything is elegant and adorned with elaborate detail. As per usual, everything will be deducted from my wages. I have money pouring in, though, so that's no longer cause for concern. I feel free. I'm no longer poor and now I have physical reminders of that fact. Reminders of my wealth now manifest themselves in all the precious objects in my room. Olai is my lucky charm. He's got a knack for managing finances and business; he makes the money multiply with seemingly no effort.

A few days ago, there was a knock at my door in the middle of the night. I had just laid down to rest and wondered who would be out at this time. I opened the door to see Olai's face, smiling at me. I had long since given up hope that he would fall in love with me, so this could hardly be a proposal. There had to be another reason for his visit.

"What in the Lord's name do you want at this hour, dear Olai?" I asked as I looked out onto the street. It was drizzling and the drops of water glistened on the rim of his hat.

"Let me in and I'll tell you," he slurred in a suspiciously soft tone of voice. He leaned forwards and exhaled straight into my face. His breath reeked of alcohol.

"No! Come back tomorrow, please. Tomorrow …" I begged, exhausted after a long day with plenty of customers.

"Give me five minutes!" he pleaded.

"No! Please …" I said. "Go home and have a good night's sleep. We can speak tomorrow. I need to sleep. I am absolutely drained. Goodnight, monsieur. Sleep well …" I tried to close the door, but he blocked it with his foot.

"Just five minutes, s'il vous plaît?" he continued. "You can go back to your beauty sleep afterwards." He held up five fingers and pouted like a child begging his mother to buy him sweets.

"You loon," I said as I let him in. I would never have called him such a thing six months ago, but now that we knew each other better. I felt comfortable calling him much worse, especially when we were by ourselves.

Back in my room, he stood for a moment and admired the new décor. "There we go," he said, taking off his hat. "This is starting to look like a real room, darling."

"Thank you," I said. "Although it is a bit small." I took his hat and coat and made a mental note to buy a dumbwaiter as I placed the coat over the back of a chair and put the hat down on the table.

"Indeed," he said, "but you've made a good start. You have only been here for little over a year."

I nodded and tried for a smile.

"Time flies," he sighed and the sentiment seemed to remind him of something. He fished out his pocket watch, looked down at it, and furrowed his brow when he realised what time it was. "That late already?"

I thought to myself that he should have realised that before showing up here, but despite my aggravation, I couldn't help but admire him. His pocket watch and chain were both made of gold. He put the watch back inside his jacket, but the chain remained visible on the outside of his silk vest. He reached for the black coat and scrambled through the inner pocket, where he found a metal bottle with a cork. I turned him down when he offered me some.

The moment he placed the bottle to his lips, he began to gulp it down greedily until not a drop was left. He placed the empty bottle back in the inner pocket as he reached for the silver box of snuff. He put it under his upper lip – the Swedish way, not like foreigners who sniffed the tobacco.

"Time flies," he repeated with an apologetic look.

"Or so you think," I said with a disapproving look.

He laughed. "My dear," he said, "this is about your future. You earn a fair amount of money. Just look at all the beautiful clothes and furniture you've bought. Still, I believe you have money left over?"

He stopped and looked at me expectantly.

"Correct," I said. "But why are you asking me this?"

"I assume you store the money at home," he said, "which isn't wise. Money loses value and is easily stolen, so I've started looking for better alternatives for you. New opportunities keep opening up, you see."

"Such as?" I asked

"*Børsen,*" he answered.

"What was that? *Bössan?*" I asked, trying to understand what he meant. "Why are you talking about guns? Are you considering becoming a hunter, Olai? What animals are you going to hunt, if you don't mind me asking? Mink?"

He shook his head.

"No, no," he said "Don't you understand? *Børsen*. It's ..." I finally realised what he was trying to say. I interrupted him before he could get started on his explanation. "Oh, *Börsen*! The stock exchange," I said with an understanding nod. "I see, that office they're opening in Christiania this week."

He leaves for Christiania today. They are opening up a stock exchange and Olai has assured me that we have nothing to lose and everything to gain. Stocks and securities are the way to make financial headway in our time. Hurray! Before I know it, I'll be even richer. I feel so alive – everything is looking up. He kissed me on the cheek as he left.

April 19th 1819

Olai has returned. It would appear the trip to Christiania was a success, although things did not go the way he had expected them to. The stock exchange itself had been a bit of a disappointment. There were not many stocks available for purchase, but there were plenty of foreign investors who showed interest, including a gentleman from London – a British man Olai had known for years. He had been a reliable trade connection for a while and he had yet to let Olai down. I believe his name was Sir Ian Williams.

Olai had been selling him timber up until last year, but trade had since ceased. Norwegian timber was no longer in high demand, but Olai told me that Sir Ian Williams had plenty of advice to offer primarily because of his employment at the London Stock Exchange.

"Stock?" I lamented, thinking all hope was lost. "I'm surprised. Does this mean we have to return to trading timber?"

As luck would have it, that was not the case and I got to learn something new. My money would be poured into British stocks to give them the chance to turn a profit. He assured me I would soon amass a fortune. God, I love Olai!

May 14th 1819

I miss having money in my purse. I miss hearing the comforting sound of the coins jingling against each other, tempting me to buy something when in town. For now, everything I earn is being placed in stocks – that's how Olai wants it. He says we must take risks if we want to reap the reward, and he has even gone as far as to take out loans for the express purpose of investing in stocks. I take comfort in the fact that I still have a roof over my head and food to eat. The only thing I'm missing is the freedom to make my own purchases once in a while, like perfume. All of that will change once the investments begin to turn a profit, though.

Olai has told me I must stay patient.

"Relax, beautiful," he said. "There are brighter days ahead, just you wait. Before long, your days of working will be over and you will be living like royalty. The money will be pouring in faster than you know what to do with it."

He has been so kind to me recently. I half suspect he might have fallen in love with me – at least a little bit. I never let myself believe it, but the hope lingers. He spends much more time with me than he did before, and we eat dinner together multiple times a week. He and I spend so much time together that it isn't shocking that rumours have started. As late as yesterday, Asta asked me if Olai and I were courting, which I denied.

"We're just good friends," I explained. "Stock speculators and colleagues."

June 24th 1819

I am at a manor just outside Strömstad, where I awoke in the most wonderful room I was given. It reminds me of my bedroom at the Silfverfors estate. The ceilings are just as high and the walls are adorned with wainscoting and patterned wallpaper, not to mention paintings in frames of gold. The cornices are exquisite and a golden crystal chandelier hangs from the rosette. Best of all, my bed is canopied. It's all marvellous!

I have slept like a princess and it pleases me greatly. Olai brought me here to make an impression on one of our main prospective investors, who happens to be a rich man from the area. Olai can be incredibly convincing when he wants to be. I've seen him work his magic and it has rendered me speechless time and time again. One by one, they join us.

It was Midsummer's Eve last night and we celebrated like true Swedes underneath the blue summer sky. We danced around the maypole, enjoyed plenty of great food and drink, and played with the children. Not even the rain of the late morning could put a damper on my mood. In fact, it just freshened up the dry air and bathed the flowers in the meadow. I made myself a beautiful flower crown that I kept on my head all day. It was wonderful to celebrate the way I used to, seeing as I didn't celebrate have the chance to celebrate Midsummer at all last year when I was trapped in the smoky inn. This year, everything was the way it was meant to be. I remembered to pick the flowers alone, so as to not waste their magic, and place them under my pillow before I went to sleep. As per tradition, I hoped to dream of the man I would marry and to my surprise, I did. I dreamt about a man, but it was not Olai.

He was a stranger in a soldier's uniform. He was a lieutenant with glasses and blond hair, so not exactly Prince Charming. Still, there was something familiar about him. I couldn't help but feel like I had seen him before … It was so strange! It is probably best not to believe in old superstitions, though. I did it for the sake of fun and tradition, not because I actually believed I would dream of the man I would marry. I will focus on Olai instead; he means everything to me and we grow closer every day.

I had not said much at the dining table last night, surrounded by the hosts and all the other guests. In truth, I had no idea who most of the guests were. They were all dressed well, but I did not put in the effort of getting to know them. I kept to myself and pretended I was shy, although I did smile at the people sitting closest to me and toast with anyone who tried to toast with me. Unfortunately, that happened quite a lot.

Some of the older gentlemen made me feel uncomfortable as night began to fall. They undressed me with their eyes, which I could have done without. I was not at the manor for that kind of work. Olai has assured me that nobody will be allowed to buy me while we're away on business. It warmed my heart when Olai, noticing that I was less than comfortable, turned to me, raised his glass, and said, "Cheers, my dear wife."

I will treasure those words for months to come …

July 3rd 1819

I almost have him in the palm of my hand. It had to happen in Christiania and I couldn't be more delighted. Last night, Olai asked me to join him at the theatre, where they were playing Ludvig Holberg's *Jeppe on the Hill; Or, The Transformed Peasant.* We had a good laugh about the story of the drunken fool who ends up in the baroness' bed.

Olai and I made the rounds, trying to make a good impression on people in an effort to gather as many investors as possible. Many of them were people of high status who just so happened to be old customers of mine. We have not held back, either. Olai has spent money left, right, and centre, trying to be generous across the board.

Aboard his skiff, we have sailed along the coast and followed the fjord all the way to Christiania, where we have met with important people, wholesalers, politicians, and artists. In short, our interest lies in people with money and power.

Every night, we have eaten at a different restaurant in town and I have never felt more like royalty. Time and time again, Olai has presented us as a couple, telling potential investors that we are engaged to be married. Given what happened after the play last night, I would not be surprised in the least if that were to become true.

Arm in arm, we walked along the river and fed the swans. After admiring them for a while, we sat down on a bench where we enjoyed the mild summer evening. The setting sun hung above the sharp, green spires of Akershus Fortress. The sky was bathed in colours so warm, I almost wanted to paint it. Alas, I had left my paintbrushes and watercolours at the Silfverfors estate, which I have come to regret. I was quite good at painting and had I persisted,

I like to think I could have been an artist. It's never too late, and who knows, I might start it back up when I have time.

When we returned to the hotel lobby and made to part for the night, he turned around and said, "The night is young, Augusta. Would you like to join me for champagne and a bit of Russian caviar in my room?"

"Why not …" I said, overjoyed at the opportunity to have him to myself in a place where nobody would interrupt us.

Olai turned to the receptionist and ordered before offering me his arm, guiding me up the staircase to the second floor. He showed me down the corridor to his room, unlocked the door, and bowed as he said, "After you, my beautiful swan."

He followed me into the gigantic room, which was significantly more stylish than mine. There was a large window overlooking the street, which he cracked open before closing the white lace curtains. The air felt warm and shut in, but it wasn't long before the night-time breeze had freshened it up. I stood in place as I took in the room. It offered a wide bed with two beautiful bedside tables on either side. At the foot of the bed, there was a seating arrangement with two chairs and an oval table.

"Please, have a seat," he said, pulling the chair out for me. I sat down and he walked over to sit down across from me. I could hear the clattering of hooves and iron-studded wheels travelling down the cobblestone streets. A dog barked in the distance and the sound almost disappeared in the hum of people chatting away on the street below us. We sat there in silence for a while, enjoying the sounds of the city as we drank from Olai's hipflask.

Eventually, there was a knock on the door. Olai went over to open it, and in came a waiter with a trolley full of delights. He placed a three-pronged candlestick with lit candles on the table, after which he brought out plates, silverware, tall crystal wine glasses, new potatoes, and caviar. He opened the bottle of champagne and poured some into Olai's glass, allowing him to taste it before he poured us each a glass. Olai tipped him and he disappeared as quickly as he had come. I was in seventh heaven when he lifted his glass and said, "Cheers to us, Augusta. Cheers to the future." He looked deep into my eyes, rendering me completely and utterly spellbound. Here he was, toasting to us and the future. How romantic!

"Cheers, dear Olai," I said. "Oh, how wonderful life is." I was in a state of bliss, even before I had my first sip of the champagne. The happiness was coursing through my veins, but then again, we had been drinking for hours. Many bottles of wine had been consumed throughout the course of the night.

He moved his chair closer to mine, put some potatoes and caviar on his fork, and brought it up to my lips. "Taste," he said, putting an arm around my waist. The chair scraped against the floor as he pulled me closer. I closed my eyes and chewed, enjoying the taste. I swallowed carefully before opening my eyes and offering him a mischievous smile. I raised my glass and he toasted with me wordlessly.

Then, he leaned forwards and our lips met. He pulled me onto his lap and before long, he wrapped his strong arms around me and carried me to the bed. He laid me down and we moaned as we undressed one another. We made love until the wee hours and every second was magical. He caressed and kissed me as he whispered compliment after compliment in my ear, telling me how beautiful and intelligent he found me until we fell asleep together.

When we woke up the next morning, slightly hung over

and otherwise indisposed, he was once again the slightly mysterious Olai. He was not romantic, but rather formal and business like. Had we moved too fast? Did he want to wait to commit to me? I stopped myself from asking any of these questions, scared I would push him away.

I wonder what the autumn will bring...

August 21st 1819

Willy walks around in a bad mood all day. He has become a proper grouch in the time Olai and I were gone. His favourite activity lately seems to be shouting at me. I can't manage to get anything right and nothing is good enough for him. He picks at the small things, but it does make me feel relieved that I haven't seen him for a while, although I suspect that might be the problem.

The inn has not been doing well in my absence...

August 26th 1819

Willy is still in a poor mood, but at least I am no longer the only person on the receiving end of his incessant abuse. As late as yesterday, he cornered Olai in the backroom. Every other word was a profanity of some sort. The sound of his voice alone would be enough to scare the toughest of us. I was standing at the bar and could hear every word, which left me feeling uncomfortable on Olai's behalf. I was expecting to hear a slam of some sort at any moment and eventually, I did. A bottle crashed against the floor. Judging by the sound of the crash, Willy must have thrown it with great force.

"Calm down! Willy, calm down!" Olai begged. His voice was shrill. "Won't you please see reason?"

"See reason? How dare you talk to me about reason, you condescending pig? You're risking everything for this."

"Calm down. No need to be in such a rush."

He disappeared out the back and I shortly after heard the door slam behind him. A couple minutes later, Willy was back behind the bar, his face bright red. Neither of us said a word and the rest of the day continued on in an uncomfortable silence.

138

August 28th 1819

I had a shocking conversation with Helga in the outhouse today. We sat next to each other on the bench and went about our business. She lit her clay pipe and the bluish-grey smoke swirled around the room, glowing in the sharp strips of light forcing their way through the cracks in the door. The backyard was completely silent. There was no sign of life out there, so we felt confident that we were alone.

Helga took a thoughtful drag.

"I can't believe what an indecent, foolish man Olai is…" The smoke poured out of her mouth as she talked and the backlight from the windows revealed the details of her face, all the way down to the wrinkles and minor blemishes. She's beginning to get a hint of bags under her eyes, despite the fact she's still young. If I remember correctly, she's only twenty-six. She's withering early, I thought to myself, surprised by how much the realisation pleased me. I was happy to see her beauty fade. She was becoming a mature woman with greying hair and marked facial features. She's on her way out while I'm just getting started. Before long, customers will stop seeking her out. But what was she saying again?

I leaned forwards to look her in the eyes. "Are you calling Olai a foolish man?" I asked. "What do you mean by that? Willy's the one going crazy. You should have heard him yesterday…"

"I know," Helga interrupted. Her red lips turned up into a resentful smile as she handed me the pipe. I took a drag and she continued, "Willy tells me everything. He gave Olai a piece of his mind yesterday and given how Olai squanders, I don't blame him."

I blew out smoke as I felt myself grow angry. Was she coming out in support of Willy?

I instinctively defended Olai. "But it was so unnecessary!" I said, my voice raised a tad too much. In a softer voice, I continued, "Oh, dear Helga. You mustn't let Willy lead you astray. He's old and has no concept of what is happening. He should mind his own business at the inn. He has no business getting involved in Olai's life. He doesn't understand that you have to spend money in order to earn money…"

Triumphantly, I passed back the clay pipe.

She shook her head and laughed at me.

"Oh, no. Wake up, Augusta. You're so young and inexperienced, not to mention far too naïve. You don't know Olai as well as you think, I can promise you that. I've known him and Willy for years and both of them seek me out multiple times a week. I never turn them down, so I can guarantee nothing happens in this inn that I do not hear about."

Pride dripped in every word she uttered and shot me a suggestive glance before taking another drag from her pipe.

"What are you saying?" I said, hurt and horrified. I had never thought Olai to be the kind of man who would settle for Helga. She must be joking! I refused to believe it could be true. "Have you slept with him?" I asked with a condescending look.

"Yes," she said as if that was obvious. "Who hasn't? Are you telling me you …"

"No!" I said before I remembered what happened in Christiania. "Actually, yes. But only once."

"Only once?" She looked at me incredulously. "When?"

Why was that so hard to believe?

"A couple of weeks ago," I said. "A month or so…"

140

"Oh, really, that long? Hm. We did the deed a couple of days ago, I believe it was. And you claim to know him…"

At that moment, I realised how blind I had been. She was probably right. I could not trust Olai if he was the kind of man who just walked around taking advantage of people. Nobody knew how to deceive others better than him. He always seemed to know how to make them think he was better than he actually was. He presented himself as a gentleman, but he was just another fake who slept with whoever, whenever. The man loved women and lies. All this time, I thought he was the sole owner of the inn and the warehouses. I thought he had built the company from the ground up without the help of anyone else.

Helga assured me that was not the case. It was instead Willy who had done all of that. Olai had simply bought his way into the business three years ago and had been given the responsibility of running the wholesaler's side of things when Willy didn't have time. He had more than enough to do, considering he ran the inn, served the customers, and watched out for us.

Olai is nothing but a liar! All of a sudden, I'm disappointed that Willy didn't beat him senseless. The business is being drained of money. We're living hand to mouth.

And the stocks? God only knows what's happening with those.

Lord, I wish the plague upon Olai.

September 4th 1819

Olai is gone most days. I've barely had the chance to speak to him since we came back from Christiania. He's always on the move and rarely has time to talk to any of us anymore. All we get is the occasional, brief exchange of words when he happens to bump into us on the way to something more important. It seems like he's always on his way to a meeting, but nobody knows what these so-called meetings are about. Not even Willy, who has every right to know. We can see how badly Olai's actions affect him. His wrinkles grow deeper and his hair grows greyer with every passing day. Soon he'll be nothing but a shadow of himself.

Everything feels heavy nowadays. It drives me crazy to not have any money. I have to do something soon. I have to find a solution.

September 15th 1819

The more time passes, the more I pity Willy. Today Asta told me something that showed just how much of an investment this inn must have been for him. We were sitting on the staircase in the backyard, both of us plucking a chicken.

"Olai doesn't know who he's dealing with," Asta started. "Nobody crosses Willy without suffering the consequences. He wouldn't think twice before taking the life of someone in his way, but by God, that man is kind to his friends."

"Has he killed anyone?" I asked. She informed me that Willy used to make a living as a privateer under the blessing of the king of Denmark. I asked myself how being a privateer could possibly be a legal occupation when it was essentially piracy?

"It was during the Napoleonic Wars," she continued – when Norway was a province of Denmark and we all fought on Napoleon's side. The enemy installed a blockade against all Norwegian merchant ships so no goods could come in or out of the country. A great famine descended on the country, and the Danish king felt he had no other choice but to give the people the right to take over enemy merchant ships.

There was good money to be earned, given that the privateers were allowed to keep the majority of the loot. Back then, Willy was a fisherman living on one of the Hvaler islands. He added a couple of cannons to his old dogger, assembled a crew, and soon he was off plundering merchant ships in the North Sea. He and his crew earned a lot of money, but eventually they had to give up when their boat was almost sunk by the Swedish East India Company.

After his stint as a privateer, Willy sailed into Fredrik-shald and bought the property that started it all – the very property that Olai is now trying to take away from him.

September 22nd 1819

Necessity is the mother of invention. It's time for me to do something. I have to start being more insistent with Olai. I have to assert myself and make sure he doesn't slip away next time I ask him about my wages.

"Soon," he says. "Give me another couple of days, lovely."

Ha! Another couple of days… He's been saying that for weeks! Now he's gone again without a trace and nobody knows where he's off to.

When I came back from the inn last night, I was so exhausted and filled with such despair that I just wanted to lie down and cry. It was so dark, I couldn't see my own hand in front of me. The moon was hidden behind the clouds and the large cliff on which the Fortress stands stretched up so far, I couldn't see the top. There was not a single sliver of light to report. Everyone was asleep by the time I arrived home, fumbling with my keys at the top of the stairs. After what seemed like an eternity of searching, I found the key. I unlocked the door and walked in, using my hands to feel my way down the hall until I found my bedroom door handle. I took the key ring out once again, found the right key, and unlocked the door. The hinges on the door creaked when I opened it; the sound was so sharp, it made me shudder.

"Damn you, Olai," I said to myself as I closed the door behind me. God only knows how many times I've asked him to put oil on the hinges. "Of course, I'll do that for you," he says every time. Yet every time, he just talks to me until I've forgotten what I've asked for, same as with my wages.

I walked slowly towards the stove and the firewood

basket, opened the door, and put in some wood. I grabbed the lighter and set fire to the tinder, blowing lightly until it caught fire. Once it did, I closed the door and walked over to the oval dining table to light the candle I had bought in Strömstad with Olai this summer.

Another memory of that lousy man! If he thinks he can keep me in the dark forever, he has another thing coming.

I started thinking up revenge plots and felt myself grow thirsty for cognac. I wanted something valuable and medicinal, and I knew Olai had an untapped barrel of the most expensive kind in the wine cellar. That's the best part. He's told me that I can drink as much wine and champagne as I want, so long as I don't touch the expensive drinks. Those barrels are separate from the ones I'm allowed to touch, like forbidden fruit. The cognac barrel is the most valuable of them all. Tapping that barrel would be like putting a stake through his heart. Willy's rarely leaves the inn. He probably hasn't known much about what's in the wine cellar since he handed the wholesaler's responsibilities over to Olai. What Willy doesn't know won't hurt him. Olai is the one I want revenge on.

I still hadn't taken off my cape, so I pulled it around me, grabbed the candle from the table, and walked into the hallway and towards the main door. I entered the backyard through the gate, which was muddy as per usual. My shoes sank down with every step and I quietly cursed Olai for not coming through on his promise to have stones laid. Thankfully, I made it to the door to the basement without falling or getting particularly dirty. I found the key to the rusty padlock, which was almost impossible to open. That needed oiling too, as did the hinges on the door; they screeched so loudly when I opened it that I worried the neighbours would wake up.

I snuck down the stairs and walked into the first part of

the basement. As I rounded the corner towards the staircase leading to the wine cellar, I happened to look to the right. The area is usually fully stocked with sacks and barrels of herring, so the entire basement normally smells like fish. But the sacks and barrels have been removed, exposing something I hadn't noticed before: a crypt!

Consumed by curiosity, I walked down the steep staircase to the bottom of the crypt, where I found a narrow path leading to a locked door. I searched through my ring of keys and came across one that looked like it might fit. I pushed it into the lock, turned it, and felt the lock pop open. Both the lock and the hinges on this door were properly oiled.

I was surprised to find a tunnel on the other side. It was so dark and narrow, I could barely see an arm's length ahead of me and I contemplated closing the door and just forgetting all about it, but my curiosity got the better of me and I ventured into the void. After the nerve-wracking climb up a great number of stairs, the tunnel let out at the back of the Powder Tower. It was a direct link between the house and the Fortress.

I dared not go further for fear of being discovered by the guards, so I went back down the tunnel into the wine cellar. To my surprise, it was so packed that barely managed to get back in. Olai had moved most of the things from the warehouse into the cellar.

I manoeuvred my way to the cognac barrel and managed to tap it, although it was by no means an easy feat. It was only then that I realised I had forgotten to bring something to pour the noble liquid into, so I went all the way back upstairs to find a crystal decanter that had been given to me by one of my customers. With the decanter in hand, I went back down into the wine cellar and filled it to the top.

On the way back, something piqued my curiosity.

Amongst the innumerable goods stacked from floor to ceiling, I spotted a box of cigars. Cognac and cigars belong together, I thought to myself. I had tasted cognac before, but I had never smoked a cigar. The men tended to keep those to themselves, so I grabbed a box and went back upstairs.

Now here I am, drinking cognac and smoking a cigar. Blowing smoke rings and thinking. Dare I take the next step?

September 23rd 1819

Today was a successful day at the inn. It was just my luck that a man I had been thinking of since the previous night came in, which was a curious coincidence seeing as he isn't a regular. He only pops in on occasion when he plays truant from his military duties at the Fortress. I don't know how he manages, but he's incredibly sneaky, not to mention excellent at card games. He wins often, which is why he doesn't struggle financially like his fellow soldiers. Not only that, but he also always has something to buy or sell.

He's quite young, and there's no disputing that either. He can barely grow a beard and his pale face is full of freckles. There perpetually seems to be a smug grin on his face, hiding just beneath his carrot-coloured forelock. His mouth is fouler than most and he always has a witty comment lined up. Despite the fact he's always getting in trouble, it's rare he doesn't get out of it. Good fortune just seems to follow him.

That's why it would have to be him. Nobody else would be crazy enough to help me set my plan in motion. I was sure of it.

Just like that, he walked through the door the very next day. It was quite late at night, probably around ten. The rain had been pouring down since the afternoon, making business slow. We were left with little to do except tend to the few lingering guests, who were now half-asleep by the stove and didn't demand too much of us.

Willy and us girls were sitting in the back, talking to the cook. There was no mistaking the slender creature when he walked, struggling to close the door against the draught. I almost wanted to run over and hug him I was so happy to see him, but I knew I had to remain composed. Instead,

I said, "Hello! What a lovely surprise. I see you're out for a walk in the rain. Come in, come in. It's been a while since we last saw you, Rasmus."

I took his hood and hat, hung them on the dumbwaiter, and showed him to the far corner of the inn so we could sit by ourselves.

"What can I bring you today?" I asked as I sat down with him at the table. He's so lanky, it almost makes me pity him. His lips were trembling.

"Beer," he said curtly as he rubbed his arms to heat back up.

"Nothing to eat? Steak and potatoes, perhaps?"

"No, thank you. Just beer," he insisted. A second later, he changed his mind. "And schnapps! I'm cold as hell."

"Beer and schnapps coming up. Is that all?"

He nodded.

I curtsied and left.

I returned to the table with his drinks soon after. "Could I trouble you for a moment? Just for a couple of minutes?"

He nodded with a smile on his face. "Of course," he said, looking down at the chair in front of me. I pulled it out and sat down with a smile. I tilted my head ever so slightly and began talking. "You must be frozen stiff, what with being outside in this weather. I don't imagine it does wonders for your health to guard the Bell Tower at night?

He threw back the schnapps in one swift motion. "God, no!" He squinted for a second, as if in pain, and then he looked up at me. "You have no idea how good you have it, Miss Augusta, working in this warm inn and all."

"I believe you, poor thing. What would you say if I told you I had an offer that might make your life a little easier? When you're on guard duty, that is."

"Easier?" he asked in surprise. "Are you proposing we swap places?"

"Lord, no!" I laughed. "Definitely not."

"Do you have better clothes for me?" he suggested with a smile. "Some clothes I can hide under my uniform?" He chuckled.

"Not quite," I said. "But I can offer you some cognac."

"Cognac?" he exclaimed blankly. I expanded the offer even further.

"And cigars from Cuba. The best kind."

"What?" He shook his head. "That would be wonderful," he said, although a little hesitant. He probably didn't believe me. Then he said, "But surely that would cost me… I could never afford…"

"Oh, no," I interrupted him. "You'll find this to be an affordable offer. I promise."

The rest of the negotiations went smoother than I had expected. He'll let me know tomorrow what time I can come; he has to speak to the other guards first. Before he left, he admitted that he was worried about the strict lieutenant from Trøndelag. According to Rasmus, he was not a gracious man. Everyone was scared of him, but I could not understand why.

The few times I had seen him at the inn, the lieutenant seemed humble. He never brought attention to himself and he mostly sat alone, blushing every time I looked his way. He never drank more than a couple of beers, but he was always a generous tipper, especially when I was serving him. What's more, he has never been with any of us girls. Such a strange man.

September 24th 1819

"The person who receives stolen goods is no better than the person who steals them," Rasmus said today, as recognition that he was hereby my accomplice. He and the other guards stood to lose everything if they were caught. Everyone understands that what we are about to do can land us in the dungeons, with all the pain and suffering that entails.

It is crucial that we avoid taking any unnecessary risks. We must only use the goods when the guards are alone at the Bell Tower. None of them are permitted to bring anything into the barracks. Such are the conditions, and should anyone break that rule, all trade will cease immediately and permanently. I feel confident that things will be all right, though. The guards even came up with a plan for distracting the strict lieutenant. All of us had cause to be pleased. Standing guard at night was proving to now be more enjoyable than ever before. The guards would have cheap cigars and cognac to keep them company on their coldest nights - something the guards at other fortresses could only dream of. Not even the people guarding Lasse-Maja have it as good as the guards at Fredriksten Fortress.

I'm sitting here, rattling the newly earned coins in my purse. The signal had worked as intended. I had heard three knocks on the floorboards. As had been expected, I could hear the knocking with the broomstick just fine. The house had actually been quiet enough that I could hear what they were saying, so I had leaped into action before they had even begun to knock. I just waited in my room and left the journey along the underground tunnel to the soldiers.

I'm reading a book written by Ludvig Holberg, entitled

Niels Klim's Underground Travels , that was given to me by a Danish gentleman who came by the other day. The book is about talking trees and strange societies. My favourite part so far was when Klim was banished from the Firmament for suggesting that women should not hold positions of power.

The book has inspired me. I'm going to set up shop as a wholesaler and amass a fortune. Afterwards, I will become the first woman to join the Norwegian Storting. I have no idea how, but I'm going to make it happen. It isn't impossible. Sweden had allowed women to join the parliament up until a few years ago, thanks to the terrible position Charles XII left us in. His incessant warfare had run the country into economic ruin and, following his death in 1718, women were given the right to vote. Or rather, women who owned property and paid taxes were given the right to vote. We were the first country to grant women suffrage, even though the right was eventually retracted in 1771.

Why not try again? Quitters never win…

September 25th 1819

Birthday greetings have not been as plentiful during my time in Norway. In fact, last year I didn't receive any at all, but I knew that would be the case seeing as I hadn't told anyone. Today, though, Asta remembered to wish me happy birthday. She even gave me a gift despite how happy it made me, it all felt like a little too much. I hadn't expected any happy birthday wishes, let alone a gift.

"Oh, sweetheart..." I said with a smile, "you shouldn't have." It was wrapped in brown paper and tied with white string. It felt hard, but not heavy. If I had to guess, I would have thought it to be breadboard, but when I opened the gift, it turned out to be unplanned wood she had put in there to trick me. On top of the piece of wood was an envelope. Seeing as Asta could neither read nor write, it wasn't a letter inside. Instead, there was a white bookmark in the shape of a cross that she had crocheted herself. I gave her a hug and thanked her from the bottom of my heart.

This is the only gift I have been given this year. It's nice to know that someone out there still thinks of me.

November 8th 1819

Today has been some day. I'm still a little shook up, so I'm trying to calm my nerves with a glass of cognac. It all started with the familiar knock on the floor. I was sitting in bed, reading my book about Niels Klim, completely engrossed in the plot. I sat up, grabbed the white bookmark given to me by Asta, and placed it in the book before I hid it away under my pillow. I jumped out of bed, put on my coat and shoes, and rushed into the basement where I was met by one of the guards from the Fortress. There was nothing unusual to report. I filled his hipflask with cognac, handed him a cigar, and lit it before finally asking for payment.

Just as he was about to leave, we heard footsteps approaching. To our horror, the sound was coming from the secret tunnel and heading right towards us.

"Come," I whispered, grabbing his arm. "You have to hide." I pushed him behind a stack of sacks, and as I went to leave the basement, I heard a breathless voice say, "Hide! The lieutenant is out for an inspection!" It was Rasmus' voice and soon after, he was in the room with us; the fear in his eyes showed how unsure he was about what to do. I decided it was best if we all hid in the same place, so we blew out the candles and sat glued to one another in the darkness. We waited, hoping the lieutenant wouldn't come. If we get caught now, we would surely be sent to the dungeons.

Rasmus told us that he had been playing cards with the other guards in the barracks when the lieutenant came down from the second floor, fully dressed. It seemed as though he was ready for unannounced inspections, but said nothing as he passed them and walked out the door.

Rasmus snuck out after him and saw him walk towards the steep staircase leading to the Bell Tower. As the lieutenant rounded the corner and disappeared, Rasmus put his hands up to his mouth and signalled the guard at the top to be prepared.

The signal was ingenious - it sounded like a hooting owl. Rasmus then took a shortcut to the secret tunnel, in case the guard had found me, which, unfortunately, he had. So there we were, waiting in fear for what seemed like an eternity. After a while, we assumed the danger had passed, so we lit out lamps and talked a little before deciding to part.

"So this is where you are!" said a crass voice above our heads. We turned sharply to look at the trapdoor, where we spotted the lieutenant's perpetually stern face and piercing eyes staring down at us. Oh God, how he startled us!

"And you, too!" he continued in a disappointed tone of voice, looking straight at me. I burst into tears and sank onto the floor, thinking this was the end. God only knew what punishment would be forced upon us now. I was on my knees, crying and begging for forgiveness. I couldn't even find it within myself to look him in the eyes, and when he came over to me, I clung to the legs of his trousers. I realised he was walking around in just his socks. That cunning fox knew just how to sneak up on people!

"Stand up, young lady," he said in a slightly milder tone of voice. He helped me to my feet, lifted my chin, and looked me in the eyes. "There's no need to cry. I have to do some thinking because I decide on a fitting punishment. But first, tell me the truth. The whole truth. What is happening down here? Are you prostituting yourself after hours? I've seen you at the inn and I know what kind of woman you are, so start talking! The more you lie to me, the more severe your punishment will be."

"Well…" Rasmus started.

"Shut up!" the lieutenant interrupted. "I don't trust you as far as I could throw you. I'm asking this young lady to explain herself."

Now I understood why the soldiers were scared of him. This was not the lieutenant I was used to seeing at the inn. He was no longer meek and shy. Instead, he was strict and authoritative, so I figured it best to tell him the truth – that this was about cigars and cognac and nothing else. I did made sure to tell him that I regretted it and that it would never happen again. I had learnt my lesson.

"Well," he said, "I'm not so sure that you *have* learnt your lesson. But as I said, I have to do some thinking. You'll be hearing from me, young lady…"

So now I must wait, with nothing to do but fear for the worst.

November 9th 1819

Last night, I barely slept. Just to make matters worse, I've been enduring the most terrible headache. I spent all day at the inn riddled with anxiety, thinking about what would happen if the lieutenant decided to come by for a visit. My heart was in my mouth every time I saw the doorknob turn. Who knew what that man would think to do? I imagined him telling Willy about my nocturnal activities, but to my relief, no such thing happened today. I'm starting to hope he will just let it all pass, that he finds it in himself to be compassionate.

I assume none of the guards will come tonight, not that I would sell them anything even if they did. I'm going to try to get some sleep...

November 11th 1819

I was sitting and reading in bed, as per usual, when I heard someone moving around in the basement. Oh no, have they not learnt? How dare they? I assumed it was one of the guards coming back down through the secret tunnel. In any case, the outer door hadn't been opened when I heard the rusty padlocks open. All I wanted to do was pretend I wasn't home, but I thought it best to find out who it was.

Selling was out of the question.

I went outside and opened the door to the basement. To my surprise, I saw the lieutenant inspecting the stacks of goods. His back was turned, but I recognised him instantly by his glasses and bright, glistening hair. I could see that he was in uniform and was holding his hat in the crook of his left arm, right above the sabre hanging by his side. A lantern he was holding in his right hand illuminated the space.

He turned around slowly and asked, "Would you happen to have any cognac?" He held the lantern at eyelevel and the light reflected in his glasses, obstructing my view of his eyes. Was he trying to mess with me?

"Cognac?" I said and I couldn't help but smile. "No, this isn't a shop." He probably wanted to test me, but his polite and friendly manner confused me.

"Good," he said with a smile. "That's what I wanted to hear."

I decided to use this moment to commandeer the conversation using the strongest weapon at my disposal: my irresistible charm. I invited him up to my room, offered him a glass of red wine, and sat down at the oval table.

"This is cosy," he said as he took in the room. "You are quite the homemaker, miss…"

"Thank you, kind lieutenant," I said and presented myself. "My name is Augusta von Silfverfors…"

"Oh?" he said. "You're a noblewoman?"

"I come from a noble household," I said. "We've lived at the Silfverfors estate for generations." I explained the location and size of Silfverfors. I wanted to impress him.

"I see," he said, sounding more and more excited. "I take it you can both read and write then? And know how to run an estate?"

I nodded.

"Wonderful," he said, shaking my hand. "My name is Sigurd Olsrud. I am the lieutenant at Fredriksten Fortress, but I'm being decommissioned soon. I'm leaving in May of next year."

"Oh no, how sad," I said, tilting my head to the side. "I was hoping you would stay a while, now that we're getting to know each other."

I grabbed his hand and tried to act as sweet as possible. I hoped it would disarm him so I could rouse sympathy for myself in an attempt to get off without punishment. Little did I know that I stood to achieve much more than that.

"Is that so?" he said. The next thing he said made my heart skip a beat. "Perhaps you would like to come with me?"

"Come with you where?" I said, trying to act stupid. Did I hear that right? Was he proposing to me?

"To Trøndelag," he said. "To my farm?"

"But," I said, suddenly worried. I let go of his hand and continued, "You know what kind of woman I …"

"I know and I have my doubts, seeing as I know so little about you. I would like to know more. Why did you decide to become a joy girl?"

The question overwhelmed me so much that I began to cry. I looked down at the table as I heard myself begin to

160

tell the story. The words flowed from my mouth as though they were everything I had wanted to say from the moment I was born until right now. I even revealed my naïve dreams to him, half-expecting him to laugh at them. But the laughter never came. The story touched him.

When I looked up at him, there were tears behind his glasses. Then he rose from his chair and got down on his knees by my side. "Dearest Augusta. Will you marry me?"

"Is this a joke?" I said, thinking it was too good to be true. Still, I continued, "Do you really want to marry me, dear lieutenant? Is this a serious proposition?"

"Of course it is," he said. "If you want me, that is."

"Of course I do," I said, stroking his cheek. He took my hand in his rough fist and kissed it. We stayed in my room for a while as he told me more about himself. He was the heir to a large farm near Trondheim, which was at present run by his older half-brother. This half-brother of his had also served at the Fortress back in his day. He took part in the War of 1814 and apparently knew Willy quite well.

Lieutenant Olsrud had no sympathy for Willy, however; he couldn't stand him. The lieutenant thought Willy to be a slick businessman who took advantage of women. He told me that he had always admired me. For months he had come to the inn and looked at me but couldn't muster the courage to strike up a conversation. He had always been shy and quiet around women. He had never even had a girlfriend.

The lieutenant was outraged when I told him I hadn't been paid in months and that that was why I had started selling stolen goods to the soldiers.

"If that's what led to it," he said, "I understand completely. Nevertheless, I would advise you to stop the business immediately. I'm worried about both you and my soldiers. It is far too risky and I would hate for anything to happen to you. So I beg you, stop while the going is good. You have a bright future ahead of you as a respectable housewife on my farm. Nobody will ever know of the life you led in Fredrikshald. You will have everything your heart desires."

In spite of his encouragements, I still felt a little unsettled. I couldn't understand why he was so willing to overlook the line of work I was in and so I voiced my concerns.

"Oh, dear Augusta," he started, almost resigned. "Of course I'm willing to overlook this. When it comes to theft, it is said that the person who receives stolen goods is no better than the person who steals them. But when it comes to prostitution, I only blame the customers and the pimps. In my eyes, those are the true criminals. If only you could have seen how much it upset me that such a beautiful and educated woman such as yourself ended up at that dirty inn. Oh, how I've wanted to free you this whole time! It was all I wanted, but my courage failed me time and time again. Things will be fine now, my dear. We will leave this place in May and leave our pasts behind us."

His response settled everything for me. It doesn't matter that I'm not in love with him. He will be more like a father to me. Unlike my so-called father, he will care for and protect me. The fact that he's a fair bit older than me is no deterrent. Although he's no Prince Charming, he looks much better than Bert Holgerson.

In fact, now that I think about it, I realise he looks a lot like the man I dreamt about on Midsummer's Eve, with his blond hair, glasses, and a lieutenant's uniform...

How strange. Did I really dream of the man I would marry?

December 8th 1819

It's almost Christmas Eve, but I barely have any money to celebrate properly. I want to buy Sigurd a gift, so I might start selling the stolen goods again. Rasmus came to see me the other day and he had the weirdest smile on his face. It seemed as though he had a question on his mind.

"What are you thinking about?" I asked him.

"I don't know…" he said hesitantly. "I think the lieutenant might be in love with you. Did you know?"

"Is that so?" I said, trying to act like I had no idea. "I would think that rather odd. Has he said anything?"

"Not exactly," he said, "but he's been asking about you ever since we left the basement that night. So much so that it got me thinking. All of us guards barely recognise him, Augusta. He used to be so strict and merciless. I don't think we ever saw him smile, mainly because he was so busy trying to scold us for any shortcomings. We avoided him like the plague. But if you could see him now! There's always a smile on his face and he doesn't pay a wink of attention to any of us. He even overlooks clear deviations." Rasmus stopped. "Be honest," he continued, "what have you done to him? I promise I won't tell anyone else."

"You promise?" I decided to tell him. "On your honour?"

He grabbed my hand. "Of course! You can trust me."

"I don't know what to tell you…" I changed my mind. I couldn't bring myself to divulge him that we were engaged to be married. "I guess you could say we've become good friends…" And that was more than enough for Rasmus.

"Excellent!" he exclaimed. "You have him in the palm of your hand. If that's the case, then can't you sell me some stuff? For old times' sake?"

He looked at me with puppy dog eyes and I couldn't find it in myself to say no. "I'm only doing it for you. Now be careful and don't get lost."

I hear the knocking on the floor now.

Rasmus has arrived.

December 15th 1819

I haven't seen Olai in months and my wages are still yet to be paid. Thankfully, I have the cognac and cigars to keep my head above water. Many little strokes fell great oaks. I hadn't intended to start back up in this business after Sigurd came into my life. I was just going to sell to Rasmus, but it wasn't long before others started asking. Now it seems I'm selling more than ever before.

Although none of the soldiers pay much, it adds up. I can afford to buy the essentials again and my home is finally starting to feel ready for Christmas. I even managed to buy a lovely silk scarf for Sigurd.

Oh, Sigurd, that poor man. I feel bad that I've started selling to the guards again behind his back. At least I know he'll be overjoyed with his lovely gift.

December 23rd 1819

Christmas feels similar to last year, except things are much better this time around. I cleared up some of my conscience by giving goodies again, although I spent much less this year than last. All the same, it was wonderful to see how happy it made them and hear their gratitude. "God bless you," they said, as we wished each other a happy Christmas.

Next year, we won't see each other. I'll be in Trøndelag. I'll be a housewife with stable boys, milkmaids, and crofters. Oh, God, it'll be nice to leave this life of sin and shame behind me. I can't wait to regain my lost honour.

I would be lying if I claimed to be in love with him, but I'm sure our love will grow over time. We've become good friends and I consider him one of the best people I have ever met. We talk to each other about everything and I feel as though he treats me as an equal. We are much more like siblings than lovers.

His careful manner never ceases to amaze me. He hasn't even tried to sleep with me, but he kisses my hand and my cheek as often as he can. He calls me "Dear Augusta" every time he has something important to say. He came into town for a short visit just so we could exchange gifts. He told me to not open my gift until tomorrow, but I couldn't help myself. As soon as he was out of the door, I opened it. Inside the small box was a silver ring with a pearl on it.

December 28th 1819

I talked to Willy today. Olai has been gone without a trace for months. Rumour has it he's been staying in London to check on our investments at the London Stock Exchange.

Willy was standing at the bar, waving at me with a letter in his rough fist.

"You see this, sweetie?" he said in his deep, nasal voice. "The postman tells me it's from England." There was hope on his face for once. I walked over to him to find out the contents of the letter since I knew Willy could neither read nor write.

He handed me the unopened envelope and I read the name of the sender on the back. Sir Ian Williams, our business connection in England. I quietly thanked my evil father for insisting on giving me the best teachers in the region. It was thanks to this schooling that I understood Latin, German, French, and English.

"From Sir Ian Williams," I said, winking at Willy as I took a pin out of my hair and opened the envelope. I took out the letter, unfolded it, and started reading to myself. I couldn't believe the words on the page. I began rereading it, desperately hoping I had simply misunderstood.

"What does it say?" Willy barked impatiently.

"What? How odd…" I shook my head and furrowed my brow as I finished reading. When it was clear that I hadn't misread it the first time, I turned to Willy and said, "Sir Ian Williams is asking… He wrote a letter to Olai on November 24th 1819 to ask when he would be coming to London. He also asked how much money Olai would eventually be investing in stocks. On top of that, he recommended a tea company in India…"

"What?" Willy stiffened. "He wrote a letter at the end of

November? And Olai still hadn't arrived… According to the skipper he travelled with, they arrived October 21st."

It seems Olai has abandoned us. We'll probably ever see him or our money again.

January 4th 1820

Willy has been furious during the day. He can no longer control his temper and everyone who comes in contact with him gets an earful for something. The tiniest things make him explode.

"Don't sit there, sweetie!" he screams at me when I go to sit down for a second.

"Clean up that mess right now!" he shouts if I've gone to fetch something when I haven't quite managed to put what I was using back in place yet.

If I stop and think for a moment, he barks, "Can't you see the customers are waiting?"

January 12th 1820

I'm starting to get a little worried. The dwindling of the goods in the warehouse is getting harder and harder to conceal. When I started out, there were two boxes of cigars, each containing twenty smaller containers. The first box is now empty and has to be removed. I don't know if I dare take anything from the other box for fear of being discovered. The barrel of cognac is half-full at most and it sounds hollow when I knock on it.

If someone catches me now, I don't know what will happen to me. Willy might pull his hair out and Lord knows no one wants to upset him right now...

No, I have to discontinue this business now. Best to stop while the going is good.

January 18th 1820

I'm going mad. Will the first of May ever arrive? Time is passing so unbearably slowly, even the slowest of snails could outrun it. I've started to drink less because I could feel how much it was affecting my health. I feel my old self resurfacing. I don't tire as quickly, but I do get impatient more easily. On the rare occasion I fall asleep at night, I don't sleep well in the slightest. Every morning when I awake, I'm exhausted. Still, I have more energy than I've had in a long time. The basement business is closing in three days.

I have to be more careful now than I ever have before, so I've been keeping my diary hidden under a loose floorboard in the corner. I don't think Willy has heard or noticed anything odd because his behaviour hasn't changed. He still shouts at all of us, so much so that the cook gave up today. He took off his hat, put on his coat, and left.

It's up to us girls to man the kitchen now.

January 19th 1820

We've all learnt to live with the fact that Willy can be hard on customers who don't behave. His protection provided us with a much-needed sense of security. We know he will keep even the rowdiest customers in check and, in turn, that he will take care of us. He protects us against the men who find pleasure in hitting women and being brutal. None of us want those customers and thankfully, there aren't many of them.

But tonight Asta was unlucky enough to get one. I was smoking in the backyard when I heard a commotion behind the curtains of a second floor room. Screams that I could only assume were from Asta, echoed down to the backyard.

"Don't hit me! Do you hear me? You haven't paid for that. Get out of here, you halfwit. Out! I'm telling you, don't hit me!"

"No! You damned whore! Are you trying to claw out my eyes," an angry man's voice shouted back. Then I heard a door fly open and the voice of Willy, shouting: "You damn cretin! Are you hitting one of my girls?"

The outburst was followed by the sounds of a chair being knocked over and a heavy piece of furniture scraping across the floor. The customer let out a horrified scream. "Let me go! Are you out of your mind? Please, let me go. I'm begging you."

The voices moved into the hallway and a moment later, the door to the backyard flew open. The man was thrown headfirst onto the cobble and stayed there until Willy lifted him up by his feet, so his head was dangling right above the ground. Willy began to violently shake him hard enough that coins and a small handgun fell from inside his pockets and bounced on the ground beneath him. His pocket watch was dangling from its chain attached to his vest.

After robbing him of all his valuables, Willy just began hitting him, throwing one punch after another. The man keeled over like a sack of flour, barely conscious. Willy wasn't finished yet though. He lifted him back up and resumed his hitting. I witnessed the whole affair, leaving me trembling in fear for the man's life. I worried Willy might kill him.

"Stop! For God's sake," I screamed. "He's had enough."

Willy stopped and turned around to face me with a glare that sent shivers down my spine. There was an evil look in his eyes, as though he was possessed by an entire legion of demons. Thankfully, he calmed down a little, turned back to the man who was lying on the ground in pain, and pulled him onto his feet. Blood was streaming from his nose and was generally looking terrible.

"I'm giving you three days, Peder," Willy said curtly. "You will be back here with one hundred speciedaler for hurting Asta. If you fail to show up, I will remove you from this earth for good. Do you understand?"

The man gurgled in response and spat out blood and teeth.

Nobody messes with Willy.

January 21st 1820

Tonight marks the last night of selling the stolen goods. After tonight, it's over! I've also finally finished the book about Niels Klim. It took a while, but it was interesting. I wish I lived in the same country as Potu, where women and men are equal.

I can hear some rummaging in the basement and I wonder which of the guards is coming tonight. I hope everything's in good order. I'll have to speak to him about the gunshot I heard – or think I heard – from the Fortress a couple of minutes ago.

Oh, God! Was that Willy's voice?

Solving the Mystery

Torunn clapped her hands together before blankly staring straight ahead, as if she was attempting to look into the past and see what happened after the last line had been written. Her thin cornrows dangled as she moved her head from side to side. Her golden earrings gleamed between the black. We all sat there in stunned silence.

Veronika was the first to speak. "Is that it?"

"Yup," Torunn said. She opened up the diary, flicked through to the end, and showed us. The last line was messier than the rest of the entries, presumably written in a hurry. The ink was smeared across the page, so it hadn't dried before the book was closed.

Torunn's eyes wandered from Veronika to me, as her glossy lips morphed into an indefinable smile that was just as enigmatic as Mona Lisa's. She must be so satisfied with herself.

I had to give it to her, she had done an impressive job. Reading the old cursive was a challenge in and of itself, but managing to live translate everything coherently, without skipping a beat, was an even more remarkable feat. I even found it in myself to tell her how impressed I was and the others chimed in to agree.

"You did so well!" Veronika said. "I have no idea how you managed to read this." She pointed to one of the lines and bent forwards to have a closer look.

"It's not that difficult. I've had a lot of practice working with genealogy. I've found ramifications in both Sweden and Denmark." Torunn lifted her head.

"We could research Augusta von Silfverfors," Jørgen suggested. "Maybe we can find out what happened to her."

"I suppose we could do that."

Torunn smiled modestly and leaned forwards, placing the book on the floor beside the sleeping mat.

"You have to!" Veronika said eagerly. "We have to get to the bottom of this and figure out what Willy was up to in the middle of the night."

"And what the gunshot was about." Jørgen grabbed the pouch of rolling tobacco in his breast pocket and looked at me. "There must have been a scuffle between Willy and the lieutenant from Trøndelag. I'm positive of it."

I looked back at my friend sceptically and said, "There isn't necessarily a connection between Willy and the gunshot. That could have been nothing but a coincidence. She didn't even know for certain that it was, a gunshot. She wrote, 'I heard – or think I heard.' She wasn't sure. Willy might have been checking on the stock in the basement."

Despite my attempt at reason, Jørgen stuck to his guns.

"It must have been. I'm sure of it." Jørgen put his rolling tobacco back in his pocket, probably thinking that there was no time to smoke right now. He seemed up for a good discussion, which was fine by me. I love winding people up.

"Or so you think. I have my doubts."

"I don't," Veronika interrupted. "I have a clear image of it all ..."

"A clear image?" I said. "Good one. You have no such thing."

"How are you not making this connection?" Veronika glared at me. "There has to be a link between this diary and the White Lady. It's so obvious."

I looked at her with resignation. How naïve can you be? I can't spare her from my opinion just because she's my partner. I disagree and she'll have to deal with that.

"Obvious?" I repeated with a grimace.

"Yeah. Everything matches. It's 1820 and there was a

gunshot at the Bell Tower on the night the lieutenant disappeared."

"And?" I put a hand behind my ear, urging her to continue explaining her flawed conclusion. I doubted there were more coincidences to point to, but she wasn't about to give up either.

"She hid her diary."

"Of course she did." I nodded. "She even made a point of writing that down, but the rest remains a mystery. It's all guesswork from hear. No clear images."

I had a great time putting everyone back in their places. If everyone agreed, imaginations would begin to run loose and we'd be talking about ghosts and the Devil and God knows what else in no time. I wasn't in the mood for an Ouija board and if I let them carry on, they would undoubtedly try to talk to the spirits. Torunn especially.

She just sat there, content that Jørgen and Veronika were in her corner and against me. I was the only voice of reason. There's an explanation for everything, so long as you're willing to educate yourself. You have to want to see things as they really are.

I refused to let them believe that this diary had anything to do with that ghost story about the White Lady. What a load of rubbish!

"Sure, it's all speculation," Jørgen admitted, followed by something that made my heart flip. "But I was thinking about that wine cellar she was talking about. That might still be there. What do you think, Frits?"

I gave in. There was no reason to keep it secret any longer. We might as well tell Veronika and Torunn about the doorway in the basement, which we now were beginning to realize would likely lead down to the wine cellar talked about in the diary. I decided to play along.

"You think they hid the stocked goods from their

creditors?" I caught his eyes while I let the thought sink in. It wasn't implausible. According to Augusta, she hadn't been paid in over six months and there was something off about the British stocks Olai had promised to invest in. The letter from Sir Ian Williams suggested that Olai might have tricked them all and run away with the borrowed money.

Willy was probably all but bankrupt and the creditors must have been ready to claim anything of value. They would have bled him dry. So with his future in mind, Willy had every reason to keep the cellar hidden. Just think, I could be sitting on a treasure trove of two hundred-year-old wines!

The women, of course, had no idea what we were talking about.

"They hid what?" they asked in unison.

Jørgen nodded at me. "Exactly. I think they hid the stocked goods. That's why the doorway was bricked-up."

"Bricked-up? Stocked goods? In the basement?" Veronika turned, grabbed my ears, and glared at me. "You lied to me, you sly fox! I knew you two were hiding something from me. You'd better lay it all out for us right now or so help me God!"

"Yeah, yeah! Fine! Ouch, let go," I begged, wishing she would just let go of my ears.

I looked at my phone and realised it was only just past nine. The night was still young. We might be able to break through the bricked-up doorway, but it was probably better if we waited until we had electricity. There was an ice-cold draught from the window and the rain was beating against the windows. The autumn storm howled and the house protested with creaky walls and floors.

"We've found a bricked-up doorway. In the basement."

"A bricked-up doorway?"

178

"Yes, a bricked-up doorway."

"You incorrigible liar! Why didn't you tell me that in the kitchen?"

"I mean … we didn't know what to do …" I struggled to explain my decision-making process, so I used the word 'we' instead of 'I', hoping that Jørgen would support me. But he shook his head.

"Speak for yourself," he chuckled. "You made that decision all by yourself, Frits. Don't try to drag me into this."

"Sorry," I said, "I didn't mean to put the blame on you. But I …"

"Never mind," Jørgen said. "Let's go knock that wall down right now."

"Right now? As in this evening? Without light?"

"Yeah, why not?" Jørgen said with a challenging expression.

"We'll do it quickly. It's just a doorway. In any case, it can't hurt to look …"

We picked up our candles and went into the old bathroom. A cold gust of air rose from the dark recess below. It smelled like dirt, almost like a grave. The entire experience was different now that the electricity had cut out and the halogen bulbs were off. Candlelight didn't work quite as well.

"Who's going first?" I asked.

"Ladies first," Jørgen smirked, and to our surprise, Torunn started climbing down the ladder. Veronika followed right behind her and we didn't say another word. Jørgen and I were stunned into silence. There was nothing to do but follow the tough women into the darkness.

Back outside, the winds were just as strong as in the hole. The iron door to the courtyard swung in the wind. It almost seemed like someone was trying desperately to remove it. The rusty hinges creaked and screeched. The heavy metal plate vibrated. The walls of the basement resonated in response. There was a draught coming from every direction and it felt like invisible hands were stroking my neck, sending shivers down my spine.

The flames flickered in the wind, threatening to extinguish themselves at any moment. I shielded mine with my hands and registered that something wasn't quite right – the window in the basement was broken. Someone, or something, must have broken it while we were upstairs. Don't ask me how. It remains a mystery to this day.

We looked up at the broken window in disbelief. "That's so strange," Jørgen said. "It wasn't like that when I went upstairs earlier."

"I know. We'll have to look at it tomorrow when it's light again," I answered, moving towards the hidden doorway.

Veronika clung to my arm. Not even Jørgen, who was walking arm in arm with Torunn, seemed entirely comfortable. We squatted down and began looking for the part of the wall that was peeling away that we had come across earlier, but it proved much harder to find in the weak light of the candles. I knew it was somewhere in the middle, close to the floor. I poked at the wall with the front of my shoes until a red brick appeared.

"It's here," I said, handing the candle to Veronika, who looked more excited than ever. Jørgen and I went to fetch the spades in the corner of the basement.

"Time to get to work, my friend," I said and offered him a high-five before we stuck the spades into the dirt floor. It was thick, but easy to dig into. Before long, we had managed to dig a reasonably big hole, so Jørgen grabbed a sledgehammer and jumped down.

He swung it at the wall to the best of his ability. The fact that he was slightly hindered by the tightness of the space didn't make a huge difference – he was a strong man and I was impressed with the amount of force in each swing. The sledgehammer sank deeper into the wall with each blow. There wasn't a lot of resistance and the reverb was surprisingly dull. It sounded more like he was hitting wood than brick.

"What the hell is this?" I said with a sceptical look.

He scratched the back of his neck.

"So weird," he said as he leaned forward to have a closer look. He soon concluded, "It's a wall of logs." The wall was made from stacked logs and clay with a layer of mortar on top. If I was remembering correctly, that was a common building method in Norway and Sweden in the nineteenth century, especially in areas with a lot of sawmills. My uncle had an outhouse at his farm from the same time period and I remember being surprised when he showed me the construction. Growing up, I was taught to associate clay huts with so-called third-world countries, not Norway.

It didn't take long for the entire wall to give in. The logs fell over with a loud crash and left behind an arched doorway. A cloud of smoke engulfed us, making the air grey and dense. We coughed and spluttered until the cloud eventually settled on the ground.

"Give me a light," I said, turning to Veronika. She handed me one of the candles and I used it to illuminate the doorway. There was still a lot of dust swirling in the air, but I could still see the outline of a staircase and a bunch of logs.

"Can you see anything?" Veronika asked.

"A staircase."

"Let me have a look!"

Nobody wanted to stay behind on their own and we were all equally eager to see what lie ahead, so we agreed it was best to stick together. One by one, we climbed through the doorway and up the narrow staircase. It was just wide enough for one person. Whereas the walls were made of natural stone, the ceiling was made of brick, just like the steep staircase. Some of the steps were dangerously worn and difficult to walk on. I pushed the logs to the side with my feet as I walked down, holding the candle out in front of me. Veronika clung to me from the back.

The light of the candle was practically trapped by the dust and we couldn't see more than two metres ahead, if that. Jørgen and Torunn were right behind us and I began to feel more and more anxious. I couldn't breathe and my throat tightened as I listened to the howling of the wind behind us. I could still hear the shaking of the iron door, not to mention the creaking and the metallic banging like a huge church bell. The dead bells are chiming, I thought sarcastically to myself. The air grew colder the further down we went and the walls grew sweaty with moisture. At least we were starting to see clearer. Suddenly, I saw something dark at the end of the staircase. It looked like a wooden wall of some sort, but I couldn't make out exactly what it was from where we were. It turned out to be a stack of furniture creating an impenetrable barrier. I stopped.

"What's happening?" Jørgen asked.

"The hallway's stacked with furniture."

"So clear them, buddy."

"I'll try," I said, trying to decide where to begin. The stacked furniture was in a sort of front room that was bigger than the small hallway we had been in so far. It was just large enough that someone had managed to bring in a wardrobe and a bed, on top of which was an oval table turned upside down. Between the legs of the table were four chairs. Behind the barricade, I could see an arched doorway. I thought to myself that if I took away the chairs, I should be able to climb over the bed and between the table legs.

"Step back," I said to the others as I reached for the nearest chair and passed it to Veronika. "Grab this!"

The chairs felt almost sticky, thanks to the fact that they were covered in black mould. They reeked of old basement. Veronika grimaced as she took the chair off my hands. I didn't blame her, although I did note how much this furniture could be worth if we restored it and sold it at an auction.

"Chair incoming." She passed it on.

I grabbed the next one and handed it to her. "Be careful, darling. These are antiques. We're talking two hundred-year-old furniture."

Once the chairs were taken down, there was space enough to move. I climbed over the bed, between the table legs, and past the two remaining chairs. I reached the wardrobe to the left of the bed. It was obstructing half of the doorway, so I had to turn sideways to get past, but I managed. I looked around and it almost felt like I was in a container. There were no sounds, no acoustics, and no reverb in the small space.

At less than an arm's length away, there were barrels and boxes stacked from ground to ceiling. Everything seemed to be in as terrible a condition as the furniture in the front room. It was all overrun with black mould, but I thought to myself that the wine had probably kept well at the very least. I'd heard about a bottle of French wine from the late eighteenth century that was sold for around four hundred thousand kroner at an auction. There might be a lot of money in this old wine.

"Woah!" Veronika said as she entered the room. "Have you ever seen anything like it?"

Torunn entered right behind her. "Oh, my God! Everything's intact ..."

But that didn't last long. Just then, we heard a loud creak, followed by a crashing sound, from the front room. A voice suddenly shouted, "Damn it!"

Just then, the wardrobe by the doorway started moving and Jørgen squeezed himself into the room. He looked apologetic. "Sorry, buddy. The bed broke. I …"

"That's fine. Let's just be extra careful from now on." I had to make sure he didn't break anything else, like a bottle of wine that could be worth half a million. He was like a bull in a china shop. Big and clumsy.

I walked further into the room and the others followed suit until we reached the wine cellar itself. All I wanted to do was jump for joy, in spite of how dark and scary it was in there. The walls on either side had shelves filled with wine and everything seemed to be intact. A veritable treasure trove. I'm going to be a millionaire, I thought to myself.

"Something isn't right," Torunn said.

"What?" I asked.

She walked to the end of the room. The cognac barrel was lying on the floor, which it shouldn't be. I remembered the diary said it was in a niche, but the niche was gone.

"Where's the niche?" I looked at the others just in time to see Jørgen burst into a sprint straight towards the wall, like a police officer trying to kick in a door on the telly.

He hit the wall at full force and it gave in, crashing down just like the wall of logs upstairs, albeit even quicker. The cloud of smoke floated towards us and while Jørgen stayed standing in the midst of the grey, the rest of us jumped back. Soon after, he emerged with a cough, covering his mouth with his hands.

"What the hell were you thinking? Have you gone completely mad?" I shouted. I had feared the worst when I saw him run between the old wooden shelves like a great, big elephant. I had seen some horrible videos of what can happen if you bump into shelves. They can easily come crashing down like a house of cards, crushing you in the process.

Thankfully for all of us, that didn't happen here. I was relieved, though slightly puzzled, but quickly realised why he had chosen to run at the wall like that. A fraction of a second before he hit the wall, I had seen that it was on the brink of falling apart as it was. The plasterwork was peeling off and there were huge gaps between the logs.

A blood-curling scream erupted from the women, scaring me half to death. Behind the cloud of dust, we began to see the outline of something that almost blended into the wall. Dark eye sockets on a pale face.

A grey shape was sitting there, staring at us. It was completely still.

"Let me out!" Veronika screamed. She tried to turn around and leave, but I held her back.

"Wait!"

She calmed down a little, but her grip on me tightened.

"What the hell?" Jørgen said. "What is that, a doll or something?"

"Come on," Torunn said and we all inched closer.

"Oh, my Lord!" I whispered when we reached the niche. On a chair was a skeleton wearing a greyish dress, or rather, the pathetic remains of what I assumed must once have been a lovely dress. The fabric was in the process of dissolving from mould. The figure looked female and was bent over ever so slightly, causing her hair to cover her forehead. Two empty eye sockets stared at us from under the light locks of hair. Her skin was dry and cracked, hanging in shreds from her skull. Her mouth was wide open as if the last thing she did in this life was scream. On closer inspection, we noticed her hands were tied to the back of the chair with a thick piece of rope.

"Poor woman," Torunn said. "Imagine how she must

have felt sitting here, watching the niche get bricked up. Tied up and buried alive without any food or water. A slow and painful death. Damn Willy! That Neanderthal of a man."

Epilogue

It all feels like a dream that I can't quite come to terms with. I ask myself if I've really taken part in all this.

Torunn had been so surprisingly certain when she said, "There are powers with unfinished business in here. Lots of pain, fear, and suffering. I see dark rooms filled with violence and murder. I think it might have something to do with this young woman. She speaks to me between her silent screams, but only when the sorrow and despair lets up long enough for her to communicate. There's business she wants to settle…"

A coincidence? Perhaps. That's what I like to think, at least. Everything in life has a natural explanation. If I'm wrong, however, and everyone does indeed have a soul that makes us more than just sacks of bones, then I think there's a link to be drawn to the virtual world.

My mind wanders to the internet and gaming consoles. When we take part in multiplayer games online, we choose a character that we control with our own thoughts. We get into the game. We're sitting in the physical world while we're moving in the virtual one.

Maybe our physical bodies are like avatars for the soul to live in. When we die, the soul goes back to where it came from, through the tunnel that people who have been clinically dead talk about.

They say that not every soul goes through the tunnel, though. Some refuse to cross over and so instead they become ghosts. If that's true, then it seems likely it was Augusta who helped us solve the mystery. That way, she could finally find peace and leave this world behind. Game over.

Jørgen and I have spent a lot of time talking about what could have happened after Augusta wrote those last lines in her diary. Judging by the state of her handwriting, she must have been fairly scared – and for good reason! She was about to be caught selling stolen goods and the diary could have been used against her to prove it all. So there was no question of why she hid the diary under the loose floorboard.

But what happened afterwards? Did she try to run away, or did she lie down and pretend to sleep? Did she pretend she had no idea why the soldiers were in the basement? Did she pretend she knew nothing at all?

Regardless of what she did, Willy and his helper murdered her. He wasn't alone. He couldn't have been.

And as for Sigurd? Jørgen thinks the skeleton they found at the foot of the Bell Tower in 1926 must be the remains of the Lieutenant from Trøndelag. I'm not convinced...

The sequence of events must have been something like this: Willy found out what was happening at the Fortress. Perhaps one of the soldiers buying goods said a little too much after a couple of beers or maybe he confided in someone he thought he could trust. Then Willy and his helper went into the basement and up to the Fortress through the secret tunnel. Willy definitely knew it was there, seeing as he had been stationed at the Fortress in 1814. Regardless of how he got there, he hid, waiting to catch the soldiers in the act. He wanted them to pay for the stolen goods they had been purchasing.

We do, however, have another hypothesis. Willy might have been hired as an assassin. According to the diary, Sigurd had a half-brother who ran the farm for him, and we can't ignore the possibility that he would have to move on Sigurd's return. A potential motive. Besides, there was a link between the half-brother and Willy. They had both served at the Fortress in 1814. They had even been friends.

According to the story of the White Lady, one of the

guards arrived at the barracks, stunned and silent. Soon after, his replacement returned in the same demeanour. That was when the Lieutenant from Trøndelag jumped into action. Armed with two guns, he marched up to the Bell Tower. Half an hour later, a gunshot was heard and the lieutenant was never seen again.

In her diary, Augusta wrote that she heard a gunshot right before Willy arrived, which marks where the two stories converge. The gun might have been shot during a brawl between Willy and Sigurd. The lieutenant might have fired his gun before he was murdered. The body could have been carried through the secret passage into the cellar. At this point, Augusta heard Willy's voice and hid her diary.

But when she walked across the floor to hide it, Willy must have realised she was awake. Not long after that, she was tossed in the wine cellar, tied up and buried alive.

The remains found at the Bell Tower had been cut up, so it wasn't far-fetched to conclude that the dismembered body of lieutenant had been placed in the barrels of herring in the basement until there was time to bury him in the ground. The guard post at the Bell Tower was discontinued and the "funeral" must have taken place in the first half of 1820.

Willy was reported missing on August 21st 1820. Torunn has heard that angry creditors drowned him in the fjord out by Ystehede. He left the inn in a buggy with a group of unknown men. Asta had assumed they were on their way to Olai's farm, which happened to be out by Ystehede. Where my family comes from…

The Author's Afterword

Dear Reader –

If you were fascinated by the story and want to see more of the world in which it unfolds, go to the Facebook page *Den hvite dame, en roman av Tom Thowsen.* You'll find photos and other interesting posts, including a German map from the 1700s where the secret passage might be labelled and a music video from Fredriksten Fortress.

Just as a little Easter egg, the chapter described in *Outhouses Suck* is based on a personal experience from when I lived on Festningsgata in the 1980s.

I also want to thank my brilliant helpers: Håkon Stang for the inspiration, my wife Irena for her honest and relentless editing, and finally, a huge hug to my English translator Catrine Bollerslev and my proofreader Anna Campbell. You two did an excellent job

Sincerely,

Tom Thowsen

Please visit my homepage and sign up for newsletters on email. Then you will be kept updated about my authorship and my future books. https://thowsen-books.com/

PS. Good reviews are always highly appreciated. So if like The White Lady, please give your review. Thanks.

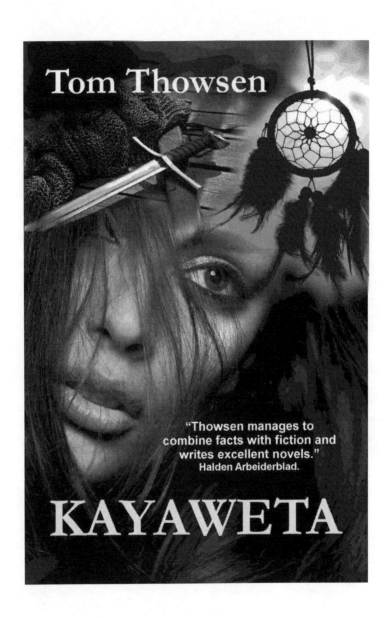

Tom Thowsen

"Thowsen manages to combine facts with fiction and writes excellent novels."
Halden Arbeiderblad.

KAYAWETA

Tom Thowsen

The Curse of Goodness

Made in the USA
Columbia, SC
27 October 2020